Margaret Sutherland is a New Zealand writer who has lived in Australia for twenty years. She has published four novels and several collections of short stories, has held the New Zealand Scholarship in Letters and has received two Australia Council writing fellowships. Her work has been included in many anthologies.

For further details, visit Margaret's website at
www.margaretsutherland.com

LEAVING GAZA

Ruth, an Israeli writer who grew up amid gunfire and grenade, startles the genteel artistic world of Barbara and Heath Barnes. Barbara still lives and paints in her Australian hometown. Ruth's arrival coincides with Barbie's declaration of war on a life she now sees as subservient and controlled. Heath misunderstands Barbara and Ruth is drawn in to fill the growing rift. But following a crisis, Barbara's future lies in ruins. Peace is a hard-won trophy — and, like her admired early Australian women painters, she sets out on the road to freedom and the right to become herself.

MARGARET SUTHERLAND

LEAVING GAZA

Complete and Unabridged

ULVERSCROFT
Leicester

First published in Great Britain in 2007

First Large Print Edition
published 2009

The moral right of the author has been asserted

British Library CIP Data

Sutherland, Margaret.
  Leaving Gaza
  1. Women authors, Israeli- -Australia- -Fiction.
  2. Women painters- -Australia- -Fiction.
  3. Self-actualization (Psychology) in women- -Fiction.
  4. Large type books.
  I. Title
  823.9′14-dc22

  ISBN 978–1–84782–711–1

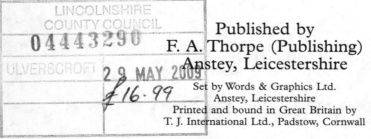
Published by
F. A. Thorpe (Publishing)
Anstey, Leicestershire

Set by Words & Graphics Ltd.
Anstey, Leicestershire
Printed and bound in Great Britain by
T. J. International Ltd., Padstow, Cornwall

This book is printed on acid-free paper

We will not go yet. Not yet, though we are now in a 'protected area' and our friends, who are not allowed to visit us from outside it, are urging us to evacuate. When an 'emergency' arises, we know that the roads will be closed to us. We shall have to stay put and take what comes.

Mostly I feel that one can face dangers at home that one could not face elsewhere. Why, I've had a bench made to sit on in the sun beside the front door in case some day I may become a grandmother. Clearly, one should try to protect one's home and stand by one's food supply. Food! It may soon become the most important thing in life.

Do we go or stay? Tomorrow when I have finished this book, I must decide these things.

Stella Bowen
Green End, Essex
JULY, 1940

2006

Israeli troops are removing Jewish settlers from the West Bank and the Gaza Strip. The ABC News shows footage of young soldiers as they invade homes and places of prayer to lead families to the buses. There is little real resistance, although men rip their shirts, women wail, and the faces of children are bewildered. Not everyone goes quietly. It was reported that a woman had set herself on fire at a police roadblock.

The images of these poor displaced people are heartbreaking. I keep thinking how prophetic Ruth's second novel has turned out to be. *Leaving Gaza*, which reflected this situation, was published several years ago. I took the book out of the library and found it a riveting read. It seemed to touch a public nerve and did very well, I hear. After nine/eleven and the Bali bombing, I suppose everyone fears that scenarios for desperate acts are a reality.

Of course Ruth, with her own Israeli background, was very well equipped to use such a setting. She so thoroughly entered the character of the fifteen-year-old Miriam that I could understand the girl's actions and had to question my own ideas of right and wrong. *Leaving Gaza* was a layered story about politics and faiths, revenge and death. As I followed Miriam's stricken manoeuvres after her eviction and separation from her family, I kept remembering that awful year when I lost my friends, Heath died and I had to sell our house.

1

1996

I saw Ruth at the funeral. At one point, when I thought she was coming over to talk to me, I turned aside to speak with one of Heath's colleagues from the conservatorium. I didn't see her after that. She must have slipped away. No one wanted to linger in that cutting wind. Half of the mourners were strangers to me; the Melbourne branch of Heath's clan. When there is a death in the family, it seems the living gather in a huddle of gratitude, our respite confirmed by each piety and floral tribute. My grief refused to surface though I knew it lurked, heavy and ominous, deep in my gut. I looked numbly into the grave and shivered, thinking of the remorseless processes it signified. Fire is a cleaner end and I wished Heath had expressed a preference for cremation. The only time we spoke about it, he was quite clear that he preferred burial. He died of cancer; that slow and bitter illness.

Helen had taken charge of the catering for the wake. An efficient daughter-in-law was suddenly a boon. I'd tried to avoid any sort of get-together but she said I must invite people, it was the done thing. Of course she was right. She was the expert on social behaviour and I thought Alex must approve of all those niceties. After all, he married her. I guessed they must have privately discussed my future, now that Heath was gone. They'd already invited me to spend a few weeks with them. Even Joe, my other son, the rolling stone, had come up with a similar offer. Alex and Joe, grown men with private lives, were strangers who flanked me at their father's graveside. Voices were low and respectful as we muttered the *Amen*. It was finished. Heath was dead and my flesh and blood mothering years were behind me. My family perceived me now as needy and frail. There was no way I could possibly explain how much I wanted to be left alone.

By consensus we turned; a little procession making for the carpark. Side by side, Alex and Helen led the way. They were a handsome couple, Alex every inch the man about town, Helen in an outfit undoubtedly bought for the occasion. The sombre tapered skirt and fitted jacket made her seem tall and her boot heels tapped decisively. Perhaps her thoughts were busy with the co-ordination of the next stage — heating the savouries and setting out the sandwiches and cakes. Joe

4

walked fast while Sophie, looking more joyful than a funeral warranted, clung to his arm. She met him eye to eye, her smile radiant. His little girl had grown up. It had been a year since he last breezed in. Now my grand-daughter was the image of her mother; that pretty, silly young thing who'd run off and left them when Sophie was so young. Joe hadn't missed the resemblance. He hardly seemed to know how to talk to a fifteen-year-old girl and strode in a deliberate way as if to remind us all he was merely visiting.

Several people spoke to me solicitously or offered me a supportive arm to lean on. Was I supposed to be in a state of collapse? The scavenger painter in me knew nothing of appropriate behaviour. I was noting details of line and colour, my *paparazzi* eye remorselessly snapping berry reds and yellows, cast-leaf bronzes, greenish clouds suggesting hail not far away. Of course I cared that Heath was gone yet my mind was noting winter sparrows pegged along the power lines. I wanted to avoid the reality of our past, an abyss every bit as dark as that dreadful grave. As for any future . . . I couldn't imagine one. I was glad Joe was going to take Sophie back to Bingara for a visit. She was delighted. Joe's latest woman had a child of her own and was willing to accommodate his

5

daughter. Heath and I might have raised Sophie, but she was Joe's flesh and blood. And I needed time alone, to come to terms with everything.

* * *

Alex drove us home. I'd been glad of their offer of transport. Driving, like all the other normal functions of daily life, felt like an over-whelming task. I sat quietly in the back seat, wishing the next few hours away. People like Helen knew the right way to go about parties, house-warmings, twenty-firsts. Her wedding made the social pages of the *Women's Weekly*. I wore a home-made pink lace frock when Heath and I married, thirty-six years ago. His family were shocked to see his bride wasn't wearing white. I'm sure they thought I must be pregnant. His mother implied we were lying about the dates when we did tell her we were expecting. Joe was born just after our first anniversary. That ought to convince her, I thought smugly. But when she visited and I hobbled beside her to show off the baby through the nursery window, her glance was perfunctory. Until then, I'd never paid much mind to Heath when he spoke about her set attitudes. I saw then that, once she made up her mind, that was that. She had that cold type of religious zeal, where rules are rules and black can never be softened with a touch of white. She needed a reason to explain her dislike of me because she was one of those mothers who hate all young and pretty contenders for their son's heart. As I stroked little Joe's soft fontanelle and held him to my breast, I vowed I would never be possessive as she was. I've tried to stick to that.

We were nearly home, following the lake road where pelicans tossed amid the white-caps like small craft in a storm. I used to love looking out over the water from our veranda until last year's tragic accident, when Vanessa Scarf was drowned. Twelve months ago, nothing could have convinced me our long friendship with the Scarfs could end. They hadn't shown their faces at the funeral and, in spite of what had happened, I felt my aloneness keenly. To be single when, for so long, one was a partner, would take a lot of getting used to.

Alex parked the car and Helen and I, black-draped, clambered out. I never wear that colour as a rule and had borrowed one of her outfits. We might both be a small woman's size but time had rearranged my shape. Her skirt felt tight and the leather shoes I'd dusted off made me feel I was

7

wading in sand. She paused at the front door and took control.

'Mum, you stay here and welcome guests while I get things going in the kitchen. Now, the cakes are cut and the quiches can go in the microwave. I'll get the oven on for the rest of the pastries.'

'Helen, can't I help? I don't know these people. They're relatives and friends of Heath.'

'You ought to stay here.' I might have been an argumentative child. 'Someone should show people in.'

I could see small groups assembling at the bottom of the driveway and staring up at the house as though summing up our status.

'Helen — '

'Don't *worry*.' She patted my arm and left me standing there. I fished out the dark glasses I'd taken to the service and put them on. One day soon grief would catch me out. Removed from my dimmed world, I conducted the first arrivals to the living room. The air there was cold and flower-scented. I wondered if I ought to light the fire. No, this wasn't a cosy occasion. And it seemed wrong to set a match to the kindling wood and logs stacked there weeks before by Heath. His ghostly hand pointed to the wood box and its residue of offcuts from the furniture factory.

He always liked a bargain.

As the room began to fill, I recognised faces familiar from photos sent up with the Christmas cards. Joe wandered in, and I saw Alex making himself useful as he passed out beer or sherry glasses. My two sons were like beacons in that crowd of strangers. A few people I did know in a casual way, as acquaintances from Heath's working life or as guests I'd met in the course of his public life. Marcus and Marian Griffin, recently back from America, had just arrived and sent me an encouraging wave. I began to work my way towards them, waylaid by consoling words and passing impressions — a whiff of sherry breath, the scented brush of a powdery cheek, Willard's bristly moustache as he kissed me and asked about his brother's last days. The room was heating up and, with its flowers and greeting cards, taking on a weird sort of gaiety. Voices were raised as hatted and costumed ladies made vigorous conversation, and men with the fierce eyebrows of old Scotsmen clutched their beer and went into huddles.

★ ★ ★

Marcus kissed my cheek and Marian took both my hands in a gentle press of sympathy. 'I'm glad you came,' I told them. 'Thought

9

you might still be away.'

'Shocking news, Barbie. Can't say how sorry we were to hear.'

'You know you can count on us. Anything at all we can do to help . . . '

They had been occasional guests when Heath suggested we entertain. He and Marcus had sometimes performed together. I remembered they had been working on several of Beethoven's violin sonatas together before Marcus accepted a university exchange posting for a year. With his long, lined face, domed forehead and untidy frizz of white hair, there had always been a touch of the mad professor about Marcus. He was a born joker but now he wore the sad expression that always settled on his features when he was lost in performing. Marian was one of those quiet, committed Christians who never attempt to proselytise but live by the tenets of their faith. I knew I could depend on her for support. I had only to ask. How could I explain to them both how distant I felt; how impossible it was for me to express grief at present? I changed the subject.

'When did you get back? It hardly seems any time since you were telling us your travel plans.'

'Yes, at that dinner of yours. Must be a year ago? Your writer friend was telling us about

Israel. Interesting woman . . . Ruth Pokroy, I think her name was?'

'I noticed her at the funeral,' added Marian. 'We said hello. She said she wasn't living in Newcastle now.'

'She moved to Sydney. So, did you get to see the Holy Land?'

'Unfortunately, no. Marcus would have risked it if I'd really pressed him but there was the usual unrest. In the end we settled for America. We could only scratch the surface, naturally.'

Marcus began to warm to a description of a disastrous campervan vacation and I was relieved. One can only stand so much sympathy.

Helen called everyone through to the dining room where a generous spread awaited. As cups and plates rattled and the din increased, Sophie beckoned me. She wore her most disgruntled face as we stepped into the music room.

'Who are all these gross people, Nan? Where have they come from?'

'They're Heath's relatives. Most of them live in Melbourne.'

'A walrus called Willard practically ordered me to put on a concert for them. *So you're the little prima donna?* Yuck!'

'Your grandfather was proud of you. You

know that. I expect he told people how well you played piano.'

'I'm not a performing monkey!'

'We must simply put up with this, Sophie. People have travelled a long way and they need to farewell Heath too.'

'Poor Nan! You must hate all this fuss.'

'It's what has to happen.' Actually, I knew Helen was quite right. One can't reject the social customs of one's own place and time. The formal acknowledgement of graduations, weddings, births and deaths dignified the flurries in life's quiet stream. 'This will soon be done with and you can get packed up. You do want to go with Joe?' I knew she did.

'Won't you be lonely?'

For the first time all day, tears filled my eyes. I knew I had only to say I wanted her to stay and she would give up her precious time with her father. 'I need some time alone. But I promise I'll come up and pay you all a visit soon.'

Unburdened, she gave me a quick hug. 'Nan, I will play, but only if you want.'

'Heath would have liked that.'

★   ★   ★

Sophie's willingness helped jolt me into a small show of my own. I waited until the

12

interest in the eats and drinks had waned, then stepped forward. I thanked people for coming and spoke briefly about Heath. I acknowledged his long career in music, his stoical acceptance of illness, his lack of complaint right up to the end. I explained that Sophie had been his star pupil, mentioning her recent music awards and future plans to study at the conservatorium when she finished school. Success was a pleasant topic and people surged into the music room, where the grand piano stood forlorn as a pet whose owner has gone on a long vacation. Sophie seemed calm. Only I, knowing her so well, felt she was nervous. No doubt she wanted to impress her father. She didn't need sheet music. Adjusting the stool, she composed herself before the keyboard.

A silence must be heard before it may be broken. When the room was quite still, she raised her hands. An elegant and stately sarabande stepped out. In its measured bars I heard a note of merriment; Heath and Sophie were never solemn, even when taken up with the rigors of advanced examination study. I'd hear peals of laughter sometimes.

She played for ten minutes, avoiding the *bravura* she could employ to such effect in *eisteddfods*. A fledgling professional, she judged both mood and capacity of her audience. After

13

Schumann's delicate *Traumerei* there was a Chopin waltz in minor key. As the haunting notes faded, her eyes sought Joe. He was applauding warmly but she didn't return his smile; she lowered the piano fall before she stood up. I had never seen a pianist do that at the end of a performance. There were tears in her eyes. She must have just realised her grandfather and mentor was dead.

★   ★   ★

Joe and Sophie, with a six or seven hour drive ahead to Bingara, were on the road early next morning. I stood in the breezy sunshine and waved them both goodbye, promising I'd consider a short holiday with them soon. They had a good day for travelling. Flocked clouds straggled across the faded blue sky as I wandered up to the house. I could hear the melodious echo of the windchimes I'd given Heath years ago. They'd hung in the doorway of a shop we'd passed (one of those New Age places stocked with crystals, essential oils and hand-made cards) when he stopped and touched the big pipes thoughtfully. *C Pentatonic?* His quizzical glance invited me to join his game. In those days we were still close. I went back later and bought them for him as a surprise gift. He hung them from the peach tree. When the southerlies blew up their echoes changed to an annoying jangle; if they were particularly intrusive I'd silence them with a good firm knot of string. *You've throttled my poor chimes, Barbie!* Once the rain stopped he'd pad across the wet lawn to set them free. I'd watch from the window, enjoying the line of his long torso, mentally sketching a quick impression of the tall figure in blue jeans and maroon jumper, the neat beard tipped as he adjusted the pipes and checked they were to his satisfaction.

As I reached the door, I heard that hollow music toll. Heath and I had been together for almost four decades. However disillusioning the last few years had been, a host of painful moments lay ahead of me. The illness had helped me switch off. A crisis supplies its own strength. A machinery of doing carries one along. The dying achieve very little rest, it seems to me. There were professionals to see, clinics to attend, treatments to endure, hope to shore up, relatives to keep informed. Heath's funeral might have been the climax to all that effort, but it was far from an ending between us. Our actions had yet to be unravelled. Oh, not to each other. It was too late for that. Heath had never understood why I did what I did. I doubt I could have found a logical explanation anyway. It was simply a gut reaction on my part and, whatever I meant to achieve, it failed to change either Heath or myself in any constructive way. Now Heath was dead and I certainly wouldn't get off scot-free. Hurt and bitterness could only hold back the tears so long.

The house was silent. No Sophie, swooping through her scales and arpeggios. No Heath, crackling the pages of the *Sydney Morning Herald* as he munched his cornflakes. Within the hour I found myself glad to hear the shouts of children in the street, or the grinding of a quarry truck as it reached the hill and changed down. Heath might be gone yet there he was in every room. His empty chair faced me across the breakfast table. His lime-scented cologne stood half used on the bathroom shelf. Awry by the back door were the sandals he'd mended with superglue. I found the button I'd meant to sew on his pyjama coat and the game cards from the cereal packets. In pastel bloom, his late-winter sweet peas witnessed his last-ditch effort to work in the garden between the bouts of chemotherapy. Already yesterday's bunch drooped in the pottery vase.

I spent a long time taking my bath and dressing. Time dragged until I had to check the wall clock to see if the batteries were low.

I brought in the mail. There were a few bills, a kindly note of sympathy from one of Heath's pupils, and his endless sweepstakes document from *Reader's Digest*. I used to tease him. One respects intelligence and admires talent but sometimes it is childishness one loves. I opened the envelope. It was something to do. There were stickers to be stuck, certificates to be filed and an imitation key for the lucky winner of the BMW. There were all the endorsements Heath used to read aloud to me, pretending to be cynical. *Cash giveaway! Nest-egg! Fabulous holiday!* He used to laugh at their marketing ploys but kept sending for their atlases and travel videos. I glanced at the glossy promotion. Heath would certainly have laughed and tossed the page to me. *Almanac of the Uncanny*. No, not really his style.

He'd tossed out mystery along with his Catholic upbringing. His family blamed me; to those certain minds I'd weaned him from the fold. But Heath had defected before he met me. He kept up the pretence for a while. At Christmas and Easter when we visited his parents there would always be cross-examinations about Mass and Holy Communion. I couldn't understand why he was so evasive, and asked why he didn't simply say he no longer went to church.

17

'Once a Catholic, always a Catholic.'

He would smile, but I thought he sounded superior. The truth wasn't something to joke about. I felt he ought to be honest about his beliefs. His mother's assumptions made the visits awkward. I would go home confused, with a husband turned into a ranting, resentful son.

'Why all the secrecy? You're an adult. You must know what you believe.'

'You can be so naïve!' He'd turn and walk away from me. I was just another interfering female like his mother.

When it came out, as it had to, that he'd left the church, a rift developed and it never healed. His visits home became more and more sporadic. His parents moved away when his father retired. Heath felt rejected, though he didn't say much. After that, he made it clear he would stick to verifiable facts. *Reader's Digest* sweepstake not-withstanding, this was one time he'd have sent the envelope marked NO. He didn't want to hear about ESP, telepathy, near-death experiences. He had one definition for the occult and supernatural. *Hocus-pocus!* I could watch TV shows about hauntings and mysterious visitors from outer space if I liked. He would remove himself, pointedly, to read or work at his computer.

Yet a certain amount of illusion coloured his idea of himself, as is the case with almost everybody. Heath was a musician and teacher, yet he could assume other identities and talk like an expert on topics I felt he had no training in. He fancied himself as an *entrepreneur*; I'd overhear him from time to time, taking calls from investment agencies, even as far afield as Hong Kong and Singapore. They would be promoting some great business opportunity that somehow filled me with apprehension. *How would those people get our telephone number, Heath? Oh, word gets around.* I didn't like the sound of it but he handled the finances. The little bit of cash I earned with my painting was mine to use as pocket money but I wasn't invited to take part in any serious handling of money. Just one of Heath's old-fashioned ways, I told myself. My psyche knew better. Just another reason to resent him and, eventually, to punish him.

★   ★   ★

How sad the end to our long marriage! Heath was a ghost now, if only in my mind. I wandered out to my studio. I expected the orderly litter of paints and brushes and the lingering smells of turps and linseed

19

would still my thoughts. An unfinished landscape stood propped on the easel. It was months since I'd been able to work at anything more than hasty impressions snatched and recorded in my sketch book. No, I wasn't to escape him, even here. Among the art books were several Heath had given me. My pastels were arrayed in the wooden trays he'd designed and built one holidays when the urge to learn woodwork had come over him. In my mind's eye he materialised, carrying a pottery mug steaming with the good coffee he could brew. He nodded encouragingly, set my drink down where I couldn't send it flying with a careless gesture, and off he went. Unless invited, we didn't intrude when the other was at work. He'd had the last word, as always. After so long, he'd upped and gone.

★ ★ ★

I went back into the garden. *Heath, what am I supposed to do now?* I would have to forge my path alone. We'd become so focused on his illness that there'd been no time to consider me. Now I could tell myself I was free of the hurtful past and our mistakes. In time I might make my peace and his spectre would move on. He would go, lock, stock and barrel . . . But not yet, not while the sweet peas he'd grown still flowered on the vine and their pale pink and lavender petals scented the air where I walked.

★ ★ ★

We met at a dance when I was barely seventeen, fresh out of school and wondering what to do next. Heath was twenty; a young man who worked in a shoe shop. Music was just his hobby then. In those days there was less talk of careers. There was plenty of work around. The average school-leaver sampled a few jobs and left if they were bored. The spectre of unemployment, lying low since the depression years, had yet to revive and haunt young people as it does today.

I smiled as this partner or another waltzed me across the slippery floor. I had my eye on the boys in the band. The drummer and saxophonist were show-offs, I decided. But I liked the way the piano player gathered music with his fingers and flicked the notes into the air. He stayed backstage during the breaks. Boldly I hunted him out and offered him a lemonade. My dress was rose-pink organza, cut on princess lines. He'd have liked to dance with me, he said, except that between brackets he had to organise his music. When he asked to walk me home, I tried to sound offhand. He was a puzzle; aloof on stage, yet his lips trembled with emotion as he gently kissed me at my gate. I wafted up the path, fully in love. Now I have to wonder what I loved. Clearly it couldn't have been Heath. I didn't know him. Was it his hands, soon awakening music in my startled body, the way he caressed the piano and gave it life? Yes, hands have a language. A butcher's cleaver says something about the man. You can guess a lot about a bankteller, seeing her snap and count the notes.

Our parents were not impressed. 'Youth is the time to play the field,' said my anxious mother. I was contemptuously silent. How would she know? In hot pursuit of what I wanted, disapproval only fanned the flames. My parents gave in. It wasn't unusual for a girl to marry young.

Heath's family objected. Apart from our youth, there was the matter of religion. They made me feel a complete outsider. There were arguments, lectures, tiresome visits to priests. Eventually they sent us off to see a bishop. He seemed a kindly man and perhaps saw me as a soul in need of saving. He gave permission for us to marry, providing I received instruction and agreed to raise our children in the Faith. Heath went along with all this, though I knew he was anything but a model

Catholic by then. It all seemed hypocritical to me. My brain, already stuffed with useless information (French pluperfect conjugations, witches brewing mischief), filed away doctrines and catechism answers to life's mystery. What could pre-nuptial instruction teach a self-willed girl in love? The warnings against contraception were just another erotic stimulus. Afterwards we would kiss and stroke each other to distraction in the back seat of Heath's car. I wasn't pregnant when we married, but that was just good luck.

Like children playing House, we rented a bed-sitter. Do young people still find pleasure in such simple beginnings? It seems to me that most couples start married life now with furniture and whitegoods, a late-model car and several credit cards. Their future children are a calculated option. In our case, by the time I turned twenty-one, Joe and Alex had been born. I don't think we considered the future. The world seemed a secure place and there was always work if you weren't fussy. Heath gave up playing at dances and stayed home evenings. He left the shoe shop, tried being a junior clerk then moved on to work as a street photographer. He even tried door-to-door selling. I stayed at home; keeping busy with the babies and our regular moves from one flat to another. If I longed to be more than just a mother and Heath's wife, I wasn't aware of it then.

Not long after his thirtieth birthday, Heath told me he wanted to train for a career in music. Alex and Joe were already sturdy boys at primary school. There would be sacrifices. Our income would plummet. But I was thrilled. We could both be students. My flair for painting, like his piano playing, had been my hobby. Now we could take ourselves seriously. Some girls make a quest of wealth or beauty. For me, the artist's way had always seemed a cut above any other. We could share that road. So we enrolled; Heath at the conservatorium and myself at art school. Those years marked a blossoming I'll always treasure.

★　★　★

We met the Scarfs that first year. Roly and Rowena were to become our closest friends. Roly was at the Con; Rowena (it was years before she steered Roly down the aisle) was his girlfriend. We four became inseparable. Rowena and I shopped at Fry's delicatessen and cooked up experimental meals, laughing at the old-fashioned standbys, roasts and fish and chips, we'd grown up on. Pastas and moussakas were just becoming the in thing. Once the children were tucked up for the night, we'd sit round till all hours, drinking cheap wine and talking. For a couple of months before Roly and Rowena left for Europe, they stayed with us. While they were away we pored over their letters and the boys begged the foreign stamps. Their travels didn't change anything. When they finally came home, we simply picked up where we'd left off.

I sensed though that Roly felt at a loose end. According to Heath, he wasn't really academic and his musical ability was only adequate. Roly was a bit of a performer, a *raconteur*, someone with a prodigious memory who knew a little bit about everything. With his huge file of trivia and a few drinks under his belt he would keep us all fascinated, or make us laugh till the tears filled our eyes. And he was a charmer. I could see why Rowena was hooked, and defended Roly when Heath criticised his flighty ways or fondness for alcohol. Our mercurial friend could make my husband seem like a stick-in-the-mud at times. Roly's surface act was so entertaining I felt no urge to dig deeper. After all, I didn't want to marry him! That was Rowena's quest.

She quizzed me. How had I snared Heath?

I explained it hadn't been like that. Finally she worked herself up and gave him an ultimatum. Surprising us all, Roly capitulated, after making sure we all knew Rowena had done the proposing. As soon as they married, he wasted no time, fathering babies one after the other until we secretly called them 'the Scarf litter'. The children wrangled and wrestled and bounced on the furniture. Our boys looked on in envy. By then, Roly was teaching at a public school. He made out it wasn't his ideal, but I thought it wasn't such an unlikely role for him. He would have his captive audience, and they would probably enjoy his style. It was true he drank a bit too much and money wasn't plentiful. But the Scarf children usually had books, music lessons, and visits to art galleries and theatres. Once married, Roly and Rowena seemed to put all their own dreams on the shelf and live through their children.

Rowena developed a passion for educational theory. She became a devotee of Rudolf Steiner and her ideal would have been to send all her children to Steiner schools. Roly did his bit. The hot water cylinder could burn out and visitors might have to cram around the oven to warm their toes in winter. But if the call arose, a piano was carted in or an old cello would mysteriously appear.

Vanessa was the oldest, and most talented of the brood. She'd inherited Roly's tall, big-boned frame. Her hips were wide and she walked dreamily, with the gentle sway of a mare. I can still see her — a young woman, maturing into a beauty, her strong legs planted, proud back upright, long hair free as she drew her bow. It wasn't hard to predict that Roly would be fulfilled through his daughter's gift. Which only goes to show we can be sure of nothing. Vanessa died last year. And the Scarfs are gone from my life.

2

I whiled away a little more of that endless day reading all the sympathy cards. They were kindly-meant morale boosters worded entirely in the past or future. *The healing touch of time — memories that live on — the strength to face tomorrow —* Oh, I knew people were sincere in their intentions. Their engraved verses tried so hard to offer comfort. For me they held no more conviction than *Reader's Digest* promises of wealth. Life's gateway was slammed shut in my face. Memories of betrayal are better forgotten. *Strength* was hardly the word to describe my fatalistic awareness of another day to be endured. *You are not alone —*

Oh yes I was! Heath was gone. Rowena was gone. Ruth was gone. It was Ruth I longed to hear from. Seeing her at the funeral had revived the link I thought we'd broken permanently. Twice the telephone rang and hope surged through me; but of course she didn't call. There were a few late condolences from people who'd seen the death notice.

I tried to rest. Pointless. I watered the flowers. I picked at the leftovers in the fridge. Eventually I phoned my daughter-in-law.

'I just want to thank you for all your help, Helen.'

'Don't be silly! It was nothing. How are you?'

'Surviving. It's strange, being on my own.'

'We really want you come and stay, Mum. It's not good to be alone.'

'Well. Perhaps. Just for a few days.'

'I'll pick you up this afternoon.'

So that was decided. Weak or not, I needed to be with family.

When Helen arrived, late in the afternoon, Sophie had just called from Bingara to say they'd made the journey safely. We chatted briefly. Then Helen stowed my suitcase and the flowers in the car while I followed like an invalid. I cut off from the busy rush of traffic and closed my eyes, letting her take control. Inside the house, we stood awkwardly facing each other.

'Alex is working late. Now, just make yourself at home.'

And we fell silent, not knowing where to go from there.

She was carrying my bag. I had the flowers. 'What will I do with these?'

'Oh, pop them in the living room. I'll put this in the guest room.'

In the immaculate atmosphere of beige carpet and pale pink leather lounges, I propped the arrangements on occasional tables, making the room look even more like a *Better Homes and Gardens* photograph.

'What time do you expect Alex?'

'Not till eight. He runs an evening clinic today. I'll fix us a snack. Scrambled eggs do?'

'Perfectly. Can I help?'

'You go and sit down. I can manage.'

I sensed life as it must become when one is a dependent relative. I flicked the pages of a glossy magazine until summoned to the table. I felt like a child again. Fortunately she seemed to accept my silence and just nodded when I said I'd turn in early.

'Have a nice shower, Mum. It will warm you up.'

A soft towel lay folded on my bed, with a new cake of Potter and Moore lavender soap. In the white-tiled shower recess I shivered, wishing for my old, deep bathtub.

On the bedside table, my clock, torch and library book looked as disowned as objects at a lost property office. I unpacked and hung up my clothes. The bed had the forbidding neatness of motel accommodation. Surely nobody ever curled up there to read and munch on snacks. Helen would have designed the quilt. She was a clever needle-woman; dextrous and careful. It would be sinful to crumple those perfectly aligned hexagons. I sat cautiously on the boudoir chair, afraid it might break. I felt as drained and heavy as if I'd had a stroke.

I'd forgotten to pack slippers. My feet felt cold. I could hear the busy ticking of the clock. I couldn't see a heater. I felt for an electric blanket switch but there was none. The pretty pastel blanket was ominously light and the sheets were a slippery percale. At least I'd have my hot flushes to keep me warm! They were worst at night. Fortunately the unpredictable flooding had stopped. Stains on Helen's sheets were unthinkable. Even in the dying gasps of menopause, my hormones weren't a topic I wanted to discuss with her.

A long time later, Alex came home. He looked in, surprised to see me already in my dressing gown.

'Coming out to join us? *Blue Heelers* is on soon.'

I shook my head. 'No thanks. You look tired.' There was a shadow on his chin. He ran a busy chiropractic clinic and Helen had implied they hadn't much free time to spend together. I didn't want to invade their privacy.

'Coping OK, Mum?'

I nodded. Alex wasn't the kissing type but he sounded sympathetic and I smiled.

'I suppose so. What else can one do? It was

nice of you both to invite me. But I'm tired. I think I'll turn in and see you in the morning.'

'Sleep well.' He gave a little wave and quietly closed the door.

But I was wakeful that first night away from home. I lay in the dark, reliving recent months. I kept thinking of Heath's struggle with the pain and his dislike of hospital. I remembered his hopeless posture as I deserted him each evening. I kept hearing his words on the day they raised his morphine dose. *I love you, Barbie.* Then he waited. He needed to be forgiven. How could I let him go into the unknown, his last wish refused? I looked at his emaciated hands. They had lost all power to make music or move me but the sight of them filled me with compassion. So I said I loved him. What else could I do? There had once been love. He nodded and smiled. Soon he entered his final, peaceful sleep.

★　★　★

The sounds of brisk showering woke me in the morning. Alex opened his clinic early and Helen usually went to her parents. They were ageing and needed help with their daily needs. I felt I should keep out of the way but nature was calling and I headed for the bathroom. Then I looked in to the dining

32

room where they sat, groomed and dressed now, smiling across their muesli and wholegrain toast like a commercial for healthy bowels.

'Sleep well?'

'Wonderfully,' I lied.

'Want some breakfast?'

'Later will do.'

'I usually run the dishwasher in the morning.'

'Oh. Well, in that case, I can eat now . . . '

'I'll be out this morning, Mum.' As Helen spoke, I had to stop myself glancing over my shoulder to see who she was talking to. I hadn't come to think of her as a daughter. Her own Polish parents had never adapted well to Australian life. Her father had dementia and her mother was depressed. They sounded completely dependent on Helen. She did their shopping, collected pensions and medications. She paid bills, supplied their meals and was their buffer zone in a country where they lived like refugees. I certainly didn't want Helen thinking I planned to join their mind set now that Heath was dead.

'I'll be perfectly all right on my own.'

'Dad has an appointment with the geriatric assessment team. Not that I'd ever let him go into hospital.'

'Be realistic, Helen,' Alex said. 'You'll have

to face it one day.'

'That's easy for you to say. He's not your father.'

'Do you want to nurse him at home for the next ten years?'

'I don't want to talk about this, Alex.' She turned to me. 'I'll be back at lunch time.'

'Could I do the ironing? Put on a casserole?'

She didn't want my help. 'You're here to rest.'

'Mum isn't an invalid,' Alex reminded her.

'I didn't say she was! I just don't expect guests to do housework.'

'I'll go back to bed for half an hour.' The guest made a rapid exit. I'd sensed for some time that, however perfect the outward appearances, things weren't going well between the pair.

Banished, I lay staring at the long, thin scroll of a Chinese landscape. A mountain path zigzagged past waterfalls and trees as it climbed towards a clouded summit. I find empty landscapes uninteresting and mentally brushed in tiny figures to face that gruelling ascent with no apparent resting-place. I eavesdropped. The phone rang twice. The cistern flushed. I studied the whorls on the beige carpet, the rectangles on the self-patterned curtains. I began to count the hexagons on the bedspread. The room was a neurotic's dream. I hoped Alex would come in and have a word alone with me but he just called goodbye from the hall and I heard his car pull away. It was fantasy to imagine we were still close. One woman in his life was all he needed to run his home and decorate his arm at social functions. I had no idea at all what my son really thought and felt. How Heath and I produced two such different boys was a mystery.

Soon Helen looked in. She was dressed in that fashionable android way the young and fit can carry off. Her makeup was subtle and her short straight hair glistened with high-lights. A designer label was embroidered on the cream tracksuit she wore.

'I'm off now, Mum. I hope you didn't think I was rude, turning down your help.'

'Of course not. You have your own routine.'

'It's not that. I just think you ought to rest. I know how I'd feel if I was suddenly left a widow.'

'It wasn't all that sudden. We knew for quite a while that Heath's cancer was terminal.'

'I don't think anyone is prepared to cope with death.' For a moment she seemed approachable. 'Still, we have to move on. Living in the past was my parents' biggest mistake. Not that it really matters now.'

'They're lucky to have you. I suppose they'd be in a Home otherwise?'

She nodded. 'Of course they couldn't adapt. It would kill them both. I'd best be off. If I'm late they get into a state.'

'Well, you look very nice. You're so trim. And I do like that lipstick shade.'

She glowed, as though unused to praise. 'It's one of the new colours.'

'One day you must take me shopping. I'm hopelessly out of touch. You could smarten me up.'

'I'd like that.'

She sounded so pleased I felt guilty. Really, instead of observing Helen, I should try a little harder to love her. Alex wasn't generous with his affection and she was doing her best to show me care and concern.

'You needn't answer the phone. We have a message service.'

'Don't worry. I won't touch anything.'

After she'd gone, I lay listening to the birds outside my window. Shrill cries and whistles echoed in my head. Dust motes floated in a shaft of sunlight. Perhaps Helen had them well trained too. Why was I making fun of my daughter-in-law? She was a good, unselfish person with an admirable sense of responsibility. I felt drowsy, as though I'd taken a sedative. I had nothing to do and no company but memories. My thoughts wandered back to Ruth, and how easily she'd walked into our lives.

★　★　★

Heath and I weren't snobby but we rarely met people we had much in common with. Relatives are accidents. One may love them without comprehending their natures or sharing their interests. Take Alex, who devotes his life to adjusting bones. Look at Joe with his careless lifestyle and succession of women. Helen was dutiful and would never forget a birthday but she saw everyone in terms of a given role. Come March 17th, she would present me with a Mother's teacup or a set of biscuit tins. Come September 10th, there would be Heath's soap-on-a-rope or sensible black socks. Though he never set foot off dry land if he could help it, his card would invariably portray a boating or fishing scene.

He was at home, the day Ruth came for her first sitting. I'd received a commission from the regional library to portray six local writers for the archival premises. I'd already met the other writers — two academics, a humorist, a Greek short story writer and an author of children's books. They were acquaintances I'd sometimes seen at social functions. One tended to see the same faces in the Civic Theatre foyer, or at champagne book launches or gallery openings. Heath laughed when I said there must be a private hit list of names somewhere. Priority invitations turned up regularly in our mailbox. We liked to go. Newcastle was trying to wash the coal-dust out of its seams. We supported efforts to encourage the cultural life of our town.

But I'd never come across Ruth Pokroy. I knew of her as the author of one novel she'd had published several years before. It was a powerful, first-person account of an Israeli woman's life; a short and unforgettable story about patriotism, passion and the sorrow of exile. Her language had a rough edge. It portrayed emotions one didn't like to think about — brutal lust, ruthless violence, the psychology of terrorism and the hatred instilled into children born in her divided country. What held me was the complexity of the central character. The woman was an enigma. She could strip and reassemble her soldier's gun in two minutes flat; yet her tenderness, writing about nature or a love affair, had moved me to tears. The extremes of such a life made me understand my own sheltered background even as I knew I was lucky to be an Australian woman whose happy accident of birth had protected me from the horrible dilemmas of war and survival.

I had no idea Ruth had come to live in Newcastle. When I next called at the library, I found her book and examined the jacket photo. She looked to be in her forties; dark-haired, strong-featured. Striking. The mouth was firm, the nose dominant, the eyes forthright and alive. A total lack of compromise was the distinguishing feature. A woman to respect and perhaps to learn from? I couldn't wait to meet her.

On the morning of our first appointment, she arrived on time and introduced herself.

'Hello, I'm Ruth. Not too early?'

'Not a bit. Come in.'

She followed me down the hall, making no comment (most visitors did) about our Federation home's charm. Heath was clearing the breakfast dishes as we passed through the big old kitchen. When I was working, he saw to those chores. He offered to make coffee and, although I was inclined to go straight through to the studio and start my initial appraisal, Ruth accepted warmly.

'I'd kill for a coffee! I ran out this morning. Had to make do with a used teabag.'

'No way to start the day,' he agreed. 'I'll tickle up the percolator. Today Barbie's the worker; I'm bottle-washer and coffee-brewer.'

'Teamwork — congratulations! Most marriages are war zones.'

Heath laughed. 'They say fights are stimulating but we go for the peaceful life.'

He knew about her involvement in the Israeli-Arab conflict. Maybe that explained the military note to the chat. Most sitters were diffident at first but, if Ruth was anxious, it didn't show. Spooning sugar into her cup she began to quiz us.

'Who plays the grand?'

Heath explained that he taught the piano at home since retiring.

'I used to learn. My parents thought music was one of the educational musts. Actually I've thought about teaching, myself, though I'm frightfully rusty.'

'But surely you're a writer?'

She smiled at him. 'Writing is a labour of love, and an intermittent one at that. Royalties don't pay the bills for long.'

'When were you published?'

'Five years ago.'

'Have you started something new?' I enquired. 'I enjoyed your last book very much.'

'Well, thanks.' She smiled at me. 'One sometimes wonders if a readership exists. Publishing is changing so rapidly and the shelf life of a book is only a few months, they say. I scribble, of course. But there's nothing finished.'

'Surely five years isn't long to gather material?' Heath suggested.

'*Material* . . . it's an odd word to describe living.'

'I thought writers invented plots?'

Ruth laughed. 'I don't mind a bit of plotting. To tell you the truth, I'm fully occupied, just making ends meet. I'm doing housework privately. A woman my age isn't going to get a full-time job, even with a good CV.'

Heath shook his head in one of those *What's the world coming to?* gestures. I was surprised at his interest in our visitor. He was usually polite and distant with women he didn't know but now he sat on with us, refilling our cups and listening intently as Ruth talked about Australia from a migrant's impressions. I was quiet, observing the subject I would shortly attempt to represent on canvas. Her deep eye sockets and olive complexion would require a rich, strong palette; raw sienna, alizarin, and cobalt would be possibilities. A startling white streak ran through her dark hair. Natural, I was sure, yet it gave her a theatrical air. Her body with its heavy breasts and wide hips was full but well proportioned. Her weightiness surprised me. From her jacket photo I'd conjured an impression of someone skinny. She must have felt my judging gaze.

'Summing up the subject? I saw those dreamy pastels of yours at the von Bertouch gallery last year. It looked like a sell-out. I'm not your usual type, am I?'

'I'm not sure I have a 'usual type'. I'd like to think pretty children and beach scenes aren't the only subject matter I can handle.'

'Then my ugly mug will be exactly what you're looking for.'

She laughed so loudly Heath and I joined in.

'Actually this is one experience I never imagined in a thousand years,' she added. 'Sitting here with a celebrity, about to be immortalised on canvas.'

'Then I'm afraid you may be disappointed! Anyway, let's make a start.'

Despite her jokes, I think I was flattered. The critics had never bothered with me, and I knew my place in the art world was a minor, humble one.

★ ★ ★

We walked through the garden to my studio; a small hut, crammed with my tools of trade.

42

I was always as happy there as other women might feel in their kitchen, creating meals. Ruth was staring at the array of paint tubes, pastel sticks and brushes.

'It must be fabulous, dealing in such tactile stuff! Writing's such black and white, drab work. I had a monster box of coloured pencils like that when I was a kid.'

'I wish it *was* all light and colour. The work's draughtsmanship and discipline, like yours.'

'At least you can stand back and gauge your progress. Writing is fumbling along a dark tunnel and hoping for the best.'

'Something must guide you? Your novel attracted very good reviews. I thought it was memorable.'

'A lot of my life went into it. You wonder why it all seemed so important. It's out of print now.'

'Painting raises similar questions. We're not like plumbers, we don't provide essential services.'

She laughed. 'We can't send our account to a satisfied customer! The work falls into a void.'

'Sometimes I envy Heath, that way. When he plays the piano, you can see the response on people's faces.'

'Music touches the heart, that's for sure.

You two are lucky, sharing an artistic approach.'

I shrugged. 'Our life's just ordinary. We trot off to our studios the way anyone else goes to the office or factory.'

Smalltalk underway, I thought we were ready to make a start and indicated the chair beside the window. Ruth settled herself. Grasping a marker, I moved it about, asking her to focus on it. The canon of the head tended towards masculine proportions, with arched brows, less rounded jaw and thinner lips than typical female features. It might stand the slightly downcast pose of the thinker, if I could do something about that nose.

'Eyeing my beak?'

'Checking verticals and horizontals,' I answered smoothly, knowing most sitters find scrutiny uncomfortable. 'Could you keep looking at that pewter goblet? When do you plan to start another book?'

'That depends.'

'Your life must have been so eventful, Ruth.'

'Purely an accident of birth. My mother went into labour on the 14th May, 1948. That was the same day Ben-Gurion proclaimed Israel a state. We were invaded on the 15th, the day I was born. So much for the first thirty years of my life!'

'Why did you come to Australia?'

'You want the short or the long answer?'

She laughed but didn't explain. In any case, I had reached my decision and was ready to start my block-in.

'Please keep still, like that.' I became intent and we said no more for a while.

★ ★ ★

'Interesting how a woman like that gets by,' said Heath, over dinner.

'What woman?' Sophie asked.

'Ruth Pokroy. She's a writer. We had a portrait sitting today.'

'The strong-minded type.' Heath sounded ambivalent. I knew he meant *alone, without a man*. Heath might have learned to rustle up the odd meal but his attitudes to male/female roles were traditional. That he managed the money and saw to the bill paying I'd accepted as normal when I was a girl. My parents had done things the same way. Heath wasn't the kind of man you could ever imagine down on his knees, cleaning toilets or washing bathroom floors. He went to work, I stayed home and cleaned and shopped. After he retired, we both had trouble adjusting to the new routines. I found he was underfoot, wanting cups of tea and chat when I had planned my day differently. Fortunately that phase didn't last long. Heath took on a few pupils, and before he knew it was running a busy teaching practice. I could heave a sigh of relief and get back to my own work. He didn't mind me keeping a small nest egg of funds; they paid for my materials and framing, and gave me an illusion of independence. I didn't like running to Heath for every little expense, though he'd drawn a good superannuation payout and I presumed we were well provided for.

Ruth's solitary state seemed to intrigue him.

'Must be a lonely life, family overseas. Any man around? No wedding ring.'

'You're observant. I've really no idea.'

'Don't women talk about these things?'

'You're so old-fashioned, Granddad!'

'Boys are all you and your girlfriends talk about when you tie up the phone for hours on end. I've heard the way you go on.'

'Don't listen then.'

I smiled at the pair of them. Sophie kept us young. Naturally we had to make huge adjustments when she came to live with us but somehow, as I saw her maturing year by year, I felt privileged.

Heath was like a dog with a bone. 'Why hasn't Ruth written more books? Was the first one no good?'

'Very good.'

'Perhaps I'll read it. Have you got it?'

'There's a copy in the library.' I was surprised. He didn't read novels as a rule.

'She's not bad looking. Funny she hasn't picked up with anyone.'

Sophie raised her eyebrows in a comical way. 'Why are you so interested, Granddad?'

'Just curious. I can't imagine a woman opting to live alone.'

'Plenty do, Heath. You might have to one day.'

'Running off with another fellow, are you?' I had to laugh.

'No, seriously, Barb, what would I do all day?'

'Teach. Garden. Pick up your own socks. You might find yourself another woman.'

We all laughed at that.

★ ★ ★

We used to congratulate ourselves on the survival of our long partnership. Of course we'd had disagreements and we both had our faults. I could be vague and naïve, as Heath reminded me from time to time. The fact that Heath ruled the roost was as much a reflection of my nature as his. The world was a rich and rewarding panorama and I simply couldn't be bothered applying my energy to such drab matters as tax returns, bill paying or investing. Heath took care of all that. As a rule we rubbed along easily. Mondays, Mrs. Looington, our household help, came in to clean. Fridays, Heath and I went out to lunch together. Saturdays, the Scarfs came over or we went to eat at their place. Sophie liked going there; there was always plenty going on. Our routines suited us. During the daytime Sophie was at school and we were both busy with our work. At midday we'd open the mail and then chat over the simple meal. Heath liked to nap after lunch. I only ever rested if I was sick. I preferred to run a load of washing, iron or pick up groceries. On lazy days I'd pick flowers, write letters or simply sit and daydream until we went back to our studios.

Unless Heath had a pupil, he liked to play the piano for half an hour after we'd finished dinner. As Sophie went on with her homework, she'd leave the door to her room wide open as though inviting the crisp regular rhythms of Bach, Scarlatti, Haydn. If Heath was feeling mellow he played Schumann, Liszt or Chopin. Sometimes I liked to sit beside him, watching the articulation of his fingers and the way his wrists sank deeply into some lingering chord. Music made me feel open to him and I might reach over, when he had finished, and take his hand. If Sophie happened to wander in at that point, she'd smile.

Of course the passion of our young days had long gone, and having a teenager in the house often curbed ideas of that sort. When we did make love it was usually on a weekend night after we'd spent the day relaxing. Perhaps we'd have driven out to the vineyards to pick up a case of wine for Heath's cellar and enjoy a stroll in the soft valley light. We might have visited a gallery or craft shop or walked an easy bush track. The evening meal on those days would be a scratch affair — takeaways or a TV supper while we watched the ABC. Sophie, who would have spent the day with friends, would disappear into her room to work on some last-minute assignment. That was when Heath was likely to reach over and stroke my back; his way of telling me he was in the mood.

Our lovemaking was quite routine. We both knew what we liked. After the final trips to the bathroom and the late-night Milos, we'd curl up side by side, my arm hugging his back the way a little koala clings to its mother. That was, until things changed. We'd never talked much about sex, Heath and I. It was only when our own crisis arose that I realised, too late, how much it meant to him.

3

A few weeks after we met Ruth, Heath and I took a quiet Saturday drive. Usually I enjoyed those outings. The isolated nurseries, gardens and riding schools were a changing kaleidoscope of human effort to put down roots and earn a living. But drought was destroying all that. As we headed up the valley I was horrified to see the listless cattle in their arid paddocks. Metal windmills, instead of pumping underground water, stood rusty and disabled as birds with broken wings. Creeks and waterholes were dry. Recent bushfires had blackened intermittent stands of trees, and For Sale signs on one farm gate after another summed up the heartbreak that must have replaced hope. I felt an angry compassion and wished we hadn't come.

Lost in his own thoughts, Heath drove as though the dejected outlook hadn't registered with him. Lately he had seemed abrupt and preoccupied.

'You're quiet,' I said, wondering if he would open up and tell me what was on his mind. He just shrugged and ignored my implied question.

'How's the portrait going?'

'Slowly.' Talking about it distracted me from the bony animals I would have dreaded painting. 'Ruth's a challenge.'

'Not the usual sweetness and light?'

He was unaware of how superior he sounded. Simply because I had a way with painting children, and had found a regular market in selling floral pictures, didn't mean I was incapable of other approaches.

'It's easy to read an elderly face, or a child's. With Ruth, I can't seem to locate her essence.'

'A chameleon?'

'I have the underpainting down. But so far it isn't her.'

'Never mind. Keep at it. Remember how long I spent on that Mozart last year? It's just a matter of hard work.'

'I suppose so.'

But I wasn't sure about his analogy. There was nowhere to hide in Mozart, Heath said. My problem with Ruth was the opposite. I couldn't find her. I would have liked to explore my problem but Heath evidently felt we'd said enough.

'Did you hear that?' He was frowning.

'Hear what?'

'That knock! I've had this car serviced twice and still they haven't sorted out the problem. The mechanic's wet behind the ears. I haven't paid out for a brand-new vehicle to be running back to the dealers every five minutes.'

'I can't hear any knock.' I felt irritable. He had a way of cutting off my thoughts before I'd worked them out. And I hadn't agreed to the purchase of Heath's new car. In fact, I avoided driving it. It was too big, too showy; in my opinion, a complete waste when we never took long trips.

'There it is, now.'

'I can't hear a thing.'

'Perhaps *you* need the hearing aid!' He laughed, not altogether kindly. There it was again; one of those tiny, point-scoring comments that had been carefully saved and served up later. It was Heath who had the television set blaring until I had to complain. Well, we were both getting older and neither of us liked the fact.

We sat in silence after that until we reached Greta. We had tea and scones at a craft gallery, which doubled as a second-hand shop. Afterwards we poked around among the unsorted boxes. I found an old mirror I really liked. Heath unearthed a heap of classical sheet music. He appeared noncommittal as he dumped it on the counter with a casual 'How much?' but I could tell he was excited with his find. The shop assistant, probably the owner's daughter making herself a bit of weekend pocket money, didn't have a clue. She stared at the ragged bindings and shrugged. Heath bought the lot for fifteen dollars. He was humming as we walked back to the car.

'What a find! The Beethoven's an excellent edition.'

'Heath, did you notice that big circular mirror? It wasn't dear and I wondered about buying it for the dining-room?'

He just pulled a face. 'I'll need a hand to mend this pile. Maybe Ruth would like the job? She knows a bit about music. Might beat those ragbag jobs she talks about.'

'Ask her.'

'I'd rather you did. I hardly know her.'

'Don't be silly. She likes you. She thinks we're lucky, sharing artistic interests.'

'So the pair of you talk about me?' He sounded pleased.

I had to laugh at his vanity. To think a man of his age was flattered to hear an attractive woman had noticed him!

'You'd be surprised! Heath, didn't you like that mirror? Mum had one just like it.'

'Look, it's up to you. The frame was only plaster and gold paint.'

'Was it?' Dejected, I said no more.

Not long after our trip up the valley, there was an auction at Swan's. I'd perused the catalogue and decided to make a bid for a pine washstand. When Heath found out, we had an argument.

'We have a proper bathroom, Barbie.'

'But I love the old hand-painted tiles and the little cupboards.'

'Do we really need more clutter?'

'I've always wanted one. Perhaps I could use it in my studio. I can pay.'

'Do. I'm not made of money.'

'I will. You never used to be so mean.' I stormed out. But I passed up on the auction. Neither of us referred to it again. We hadn't grown up in the fashion of telling every little feeling.

'What's wrong, Nan?' Sophie asked some time later and I looked at her enquiringly. We'd had a minor confrontation about her untidy bedroom but that was days before. Usually she was quite a comfort to me. She was my younger self; the girl with all the options in the world to pick from.

'You seem — lonely. Really quiet.'

'Do I? I'm not feeling too bright. It's probably hormones.'

'Those!' She laughed. 'I know what you mean!'

54

I thought of her, white and sick every month, swallowing her painkillers before she battled off to school. 'It's not fair, is it, what we females put up with?' I smiled at her in sympathy.

'Oh, I don't know!'

She was coquettish and suddenly I realised sexual desire was real for her. She wasn't a child. I'd laundered her bras and taught her to soak bloodstains in cold salted water without acknowledging that very obvious fact. So far there'd been no special boyfriend but she had a private life and, before I could blink, she'd be an adult, she'd be gone. I'd talked to her about the facts of life but, let's face it, detached from feeling they are pretty dry. Her knowing tone jolted me. I began to wish she were older so I could confide in her. I really needed someone to talk to.

Rowena was always caught up with family and Ruth and I were hardly close friends. Since meeting her, I was very aware that some women live independently. Despite her financial struggle and her single state, I envied her. Heath was really no different from the man he'd always been; a little more entrenched, perhaps, in the uncompromising stands he took. Still, he'd been doing that all our married life and I'm sure he wasn't aware of it. He simply carried on as normal. I was the one who had changed. I no longer desired him. If he wanted to make love, the mirror and the washstand flashed into my thoughts and I brushed him off. A lifetime of small resentments seemed to have accumulated into a fireball of rage. I couldn't shake my fist in his face, or rant and rave. My body just closed down to him.

At the time, those weren't conscious thoughts. I couldn't understand myself. Each time I turned away, Heath asked how long the change of life went on. He assumed that was what was wrong with me. Perhaps it was. How was I to know? I said that sex had become uncomfortable. We faced the greatest conflict of our marriage when I suggested we should simply forget that side of life.

'You shouldn't mind too much,' I said. 'After all, you'll soon be sixty.'

He looked desolate. I wished he might put his arms around me and tell me that he needed me. But he was too proud a man for that.

'You'd better see a specialist,' he said. 'I've heard women can go this way. They can probably give you some tablets and fix you up.'

I flared up at once. 'I'm not a car with a knock in the engine! I don't want to see a doctor. I just don't want sex any more.'

Heath's expression became cold and sulky. He'd never had to beg for anything in his life. I was confronting him with a need he'd always taken as his right.

'You can't be suggesting we live like brother and sister?' he argued. 'I might be getting on in years but I'm still a normal human being. Surely you know that?'

I knew. And so was I. Thousands of times I'd given in to Heath. I'd compromised, negotiated. Because I'd never earned much money he treated my painting as a hobby. I wanted him to respect me and stop treating me as a possession.

'We'll get used to it,' I told him.

He saw that I'd made up my mind. 'If it's over, then it's over.'

I knew he was waiting for me to soften as he turned his face away. His withdrawn pro-file made me angry. I wanted to punish him.

'It *is* over, Heath.'

An expression of sorrow creased his face as he stood up and walked away.

For once, I was in charge. I felt strong. But it didn't last. I hadn't realised how badly my ultimatum would affect us. Heath didn't touch me and he turned his back on me at night. If I cuddled against him, he shifted away. He asked me point-blank to stay on my own side of the bed. After a while he suggested we move into separate rooms. We had our biggest row that day. In the end we compromised. When the furniture van brought the single beds and carted the queen size away, I sat on the edge of my new posturopedic mattress and cried as though someone dear to me had died. I'd childishly tried to manipulate some basic change between us. I'd somehow expected to be wooed, persuaded, convinced that I was loved. But Heath had never been that way. He was kind, he remembered my birthday, but he was always the boy who wouldn't dance with me because he had his own business to see to. Instead of showing him he must stop acting as my better half, all I'd done was make him retreat further into himself.

He was a determined man once he chose a course of action. In the same way he'd left the church and stopped visiting his parents, he moved away from me emotionally. As far as the new beds went, he said he liked the back support. He took to reading late at night. We bought new bedside lamps. He didn't want to disturb my sleep. Sometimes I'd wake and sense his bed was empty. He'd be in the kitchen, brewing tea, skimming a newspaper.

'Sorry, did I wake you?'

'No, no. Sleeping lightly, that's all. I'll join you in a cuppa.'

We'd sit there, sipping tea, the intimacy of the night surrounding us.

'I'll sit up a while,' he'd say, when I suggested we should both go back to bed. 'I'll be in shortly.'

I was the one who lay awake and lonely, tears stinging my eyes. Sex had never been the driving force between us, surely? I'd have described it as one of our many links — no more. Funny. My ultimatum had turned against myself. Somehow, long before the cancer struck and carried him off, I felt I'd lost him.

★   ★   ★

After the funeral, I only stayed a few nights with Alex and Helen. They were surprised but I said I needed to be at home. Alex drove me through the early evening landscape. At that time, a brooding iridescence glowed at the heart of nature. Grass was a peculiar acid green and the lake gleamed pewter. We turned into my street. The garden looked neglected, with poinsettias straggling and rose bushes poking gaunt stems through the weedy borders. Where irises and poppies should have bloomed there was only a tangle of winter weeds.

'Lawn needs cutting. We'll have to arrange

a mowing service.'

Alex wasn't a man to push a lawn mower; every inch of his garden was banished under plastic and woodchip. Joe was the gardener, though I had no wish to know the nature of his crops.

At the front door I put down the wretched posy bowls Helen had made me bring home, and fumbled for my key.

'Anything you want a hand with, Mother?' Alex followed me into the house. I shook my head. He might feel easier, changing a light bulb, fixing a fuse, but I couldn't think straight.

'Let me make you a cup of tea.'

'Yes please.' He wanted to be kind. What was he really like, this strong-shouldered man in his late thirties, his hair dark blonde, the colour mine used to be? The cut was neat and short. Close-shaven, his evening face with its day's regrowth looked tired. His shirt fitted the outline of an athletic singlet, his woollen trousers had a modern cut, his belt and shoes were probably imported. His clothes announced a careful man, a man with self-esteem. If he had any doubts or troubles, they were well hidden.

'You'll need a hand sorting out Dad's affairs,' he suggested as we sat together sipping the hot tea.

60

'There's a Will,' I reminded him. Surely he knew I'd inherit whatever assets we had? 'Do you want your father's watch as a keepsake?'

Alex shrugged. 'It's you I'm concerned about.'

'You don't need to be. I'm well provided for.'

'Did Dad ever talk to you about his investments?'

'You know your father. He held the purse strings. He always did.' My son needn't think he was going to take over my finances. Perhaps he had an eye to his future inheritance. 'It will all come to you boys, eventually.'

'I'm not on the make!' He sounded annoyed. 'Dad wasn't the world's best financier. He made those bad investments in Equiticorp and Quintex. He lost a heap when they went under. He approached me about a loan.'

'Heath wanted you to lend him money?' I couldn't hide my disbelief. 'But he would never borrow. He didn't even like time-payments.'

'He wanted to recoup his losses. Quite frankly, I thought it was the wrong way to go. Something to do with Futures; far too risky, in my opinion. Anyway, I couldn't help. I was up to my neck, getting the practice going.'

'I don't understand. Why didn't he just approach the bank? We had all that superannuation. We have plenty of money.'

Looking uncomfortable, Alex stood up and pressed my shoulder. 'I'd check. And look, I'm here, if you need advice.'

Naturally he meant well, talking down to me just like Heath. I spoke briskly. 'You'll be the first to know, dear.'

'Phone us as soon as you check. If we're out, leave a message. Helen's at her parents most days.'

'Quite a tie.' I meant, for Helen.

'Yes. She ought to go back to work. Instead she's landed with this unpaid nursemaid's job.'

'They're her parents, Alex. She loves them.'

'I know that. It's no reason to be made use of. I pay a heap of tax to fund the country's health services.'

That was the kind of comment Heath would have made. Silently I kissed my son's cheek. 'Go on home, love. I'll be fine.'

'Sure?'

'Yes.' I stood waving from the doorway until his car revved up and pulled away. Then I set the deadlock and made sure the windows were latched.

The chilly house depressed me but I couldn't be bothered lighting the fire. Instead

I had a hot bath and turned in early, glad to be back in familiar surroundings. Heath's empty bed was a real presence in the room. Even though his last weeks had been spent in hospital, I half expected to see him walk in, wearing pyjamas, fold back the bedspread and settle down for the night. It would take me a long time to adjust. The conversation with Alex had sown seeds of unease in my mind. Eventually I put on slippers and dressing gown and went into Heath's studio, which also housed his computer and the family records. The fall of the grand piano was down, just as Sophie had left it. A printout of his teaching roster lay on the desk. Some of his students might not have heard the news. That was a job I'd have to see to.

I located the business records easily. Heath was always methodical. I couldn't get the computer going but I found papers in the filing cabinet. I pulled out a copy of the Will, fixed deposit records, share certificates, bank statements, the house and car insurances. Holding those papers was a strange experience. I felt like a spy. They belonged to Heath, I felt, regardless of the fact that I was now responsible for everything. Making a cup of Milo, I carried everything back to bed and began to wade through the legal language. *I revoke . . . I appoint . . . I give devise and bequeath . . .* In spite of the jargon the contents were clear. All assets were mine in my lifetime, to be willed on to the boys at my death. A proviso covered the conditions in the event that I remarried. That had been one of the times Heath reminded me I was naïve. *There are con men who prey on helpless widows, Barbie.* I remembered how I'd laughed. Was that how Heath saw me? Did he really think men would come flocking to a middle-aged woman, or that I would disinherit our sons in favour of some Johnny-come-lately? I'd waited long enough to manage my own business. I had no intention of handing over my affairs to anyone.

The insurances and receipts were in order but I couldn't find renewal dates on the old fixed deposit records. There were a number of old share certificates as well as Chess statements that related to the stock market. Heath had started buying and selling in the late eighties. When he bought his first computer he would sit for hours, hunched over spread-sheets and files. I took no interest in any of it. Presumably he was just having fun, playing with numbers in the same way those animated figures raced across his screen, evading monsters or crashing through trap doors. But the large sums of money on those certificates were no game. Nearly all our money must be in shares. Barbie the tycoon. Well, I would simply have to learn the language. I'd have to contact the bank and see what ready cash was available. Our cheque account balance, which earned no interest, was always small. I wondered where the house deeds were. I was sure we had received them after Heath paid out the mortgage. I'd have to ring our lawyer. He'd soon sort things out.

* * *

My dreams that night were of immense riches. I was a queen, surrounded by beggars. One was Alex, another Helen. I couldn't see Joe as I began dispensing largesse but the more I gave away, the more jewels and money spilled from my hands. I was making an announcement. *I have everything I need, take it all!* People cheered and wept for joy as gold coins fell in heaps and rolled down the gutters. I looked up and saw Joe, crouched in a monkey-puzzle tree, grinning as he beckoned me to leave them to it.

It was a silly dream, but vivid. Money did bestow freedom. Heath hadn't been dead a week and already I was considering a new life. I might move into town or shift to the Central Coast; Gosford or Erina, any of those tranquil retreats Heath saw as cultural deserts. But how much culture did I really want? Once Sophie was off to university, why would I need this costly family home? I could sell up, get settled somewhere, and then share the residue with my children while it could do some good. I knew Alex had to struggle to meet the costs of professional practice. Joe could certainly use a hand. Sophie's tertiary education would cost plenty. Meanwhile I might travel, take a cruise. Heath wouldn't expect me to sit at home, grieving until I was a shrivelled-up old woman.

And then I began to make my enquiries. The bank informed me the fixed deposits had been withdrawn years before. There was no savings account and of course the joint cheque account was almost empty. The manager offered his condolences politely, as though he didn't mind whether I kept my business with him or went elsewhere. My next hope was our lawyer. He had the original Will but knew nothing about the house deeds. I told him about the share certificates and he gave me the name of a stockbroker I should telephone. Grasping the Chess state-ments and the blue and lavender certificates with their directors' signatures and impressive seals, I enquired how one went about cashing in one's shares. There was a brief silence after I read out the companies concerned.

'Equiticorp shares go back a long way. I'm afraid the company went into receivership.'

'But I have a transfer letter to the Hong Kong Stock Exchange.' I was about to read it out when he interrupted.

'I'm sorry. They went broke. And I'm afraid Quintex went the same way.'

'Are you saying these stocks will never pick up in value?'

'That's what I'm saying.' He spoke patiently as though I was an imbecile.

'What shall I do with these certificates?'

'They're worthless, most of them. Throw them out. You could sell the small parcel of shares in Woolworths and we could offload the nickel mining stock, though at present they're so low I fear you'd only cover the brokerage.'

'Well, thank you for your advice.'

Naturally I phoned another firm. When they told me the same story I began to realise that Heath had left me almost penniless.

Alex and Helen came round to help me face my situation. It was as bad as it could be. Heath had gambled our security away. After the failure of the supposed blue chip investments, he'd re-mortgaged the house and bought up speculative mining stocks.

They'd failed or disappeared. The rest of the money had been lost in high-risk Futures. Alex found the records in the computer. He sounded angry as he scrolled through page after page of figures.

'Did you agree to all this, Mother?'

'Of course not.'

'Why didn't you stop him?'

'I didn't know.'

'But Mum,' Helen intervened, 'they were your assets too.'

It was all very well for her to sound so judgmental. She didn't understand our generation or the way things used to be. I felt I had to explain.

'Heath always handled the money. He didn't see it as a woman's job.'

'This isn't the dark ages.' Alex sounded disgusted. 'What about the house? At least you must have agreed to re-mortgage it? You'd have had to give your signature.'

'I may have signed something. I can't remember! You don't understand, Alex. I trusted him!'

They thought I'd been negligent, stupid, lazy. And these were only the financial deceits. Did they know of the betrayals that led up to Heath's death and the loss of my best friends? I turned away, weeping, and the cross-examination stopped. Helen rushed out to make cups of tea while Alex put his arm around me. I made an effort to pull myself together.

'Is this as bad as it seems, Alex?'

'There might be some kind of pension. But I think you'll have to sell. There's no money and a huge mortgage.'

We fell silent then. Helen came back soon. Putting the tray down, she tried to reassure me.

'You can always come to us. We'd never let you down.'

I managed a grateful nod, but I couldn't help remembering how I'd felt, cooped up in that small spare room, counting hexagons on a quilt that wasn't mine.

I began to cry again, for I was partly to blame for my dilemma. The questions I should have asked had simple answers. The superannuation was gone and Heath's investments had failed. The tiny bit of capital I could realise wouldn't last for long. I had no idea how Welfare worked. I had always assumed it was a system to prop up a different type of person from myself. Perhaps I'd be forced to register as unemployed. I ought to have paid attention. Instead I'd left it all to Heath. Ruth once said to me, *Innocence is dangerous*. I'd wondered what she meant. I understood her now.

4

Ruth. Such an interesting person! Perhaps our differences provided the attraction. Heath and I lived such a settled life, secure in Australia, in touch with our children, insulated from the conflicts that characterised her life. Working with the portrait, I speculated on the secrets of her past, for many moods had left their mark on her expressive face. I never knew from visit to visit what to expect of her. She might talk vivaciously or sit in a brown study, haggard and unfriendly. Often she would shift about or alter position until I had to remind her this was a working session. One day she arrived with her hair done completely differently. She'd forgotten I was painting her. While I loosened the bun and combed it out she laughed at me, saying I was just like her mother.

I worked much harder than I usually did to get below the surface; I wanted to impress her. I could have managed with fewer sittings but they were our excuse to meet. She was an elusive woman. However open, however warm she seemed, a moment arrived when

70

Ruth threw the switch. As she waved and went, I'd wonder if I'd see her again and felt I wouldn't be missed. Our time together never seemed enough. I wanted to believe she was my friend. Heath liked her too. He was a different man when she was around. He didn't complain about his health, and the bickering and tension that had set in between us stopped. I must admit I hadn't much patience with Heath's litany of ailments. He would present them to me accusingly, as though it was all my fault that he had been precipitated into old age and incapacity. 'Not baked beans again!' he'd say. 'You know they give me indigestion.'

His anticipatory look as he placed his hand on his chest would annoy me. 'There's Dexsal in the bathroom,' I'd remind him briskly. He was becoming a hypochondriac, I felt. He'd twisted his knee. He had sinus, an ingrown toenail, strange muscle aches. All the time I was thinking to myself how he had no understanding of my own problems; hot flushes, headaches, signs of ageing every time I looked into the mirror.

'Face facts,' I'd snap. 'Aches and pains must be expected at our age. You're no different from any other man.'

'Is that so, Barbara?' He had that new expression again, as though he was seeing me differently and didn't particularly like the view.

There were moments when I pitied Heath; when I wanted to put my arms around him and weep for us both. I longed to pour out my own hurts, pains, self-disgust and fear of old age. But one couldn't confide in a man who sighed so pointedly, turned his back and went off to work on his computer.

However, those were passing irritations. Sophie often had Vanessa over and the girls lightened the atmosphere for me. We both kept busy. Heath's practice was full. He'd meant to keep to part-time work but word of mouth began to spread. With pupils he was patient, thorough and encouraging. Within a year of retiring he was fully booked. I was relieved. He wasn't a man to sit about doing nothing, nor did he play golf or bowls. I enjoyed the students too. Most were hard workers, studying for higher exams or the Year 12 Finals. A few little ones came, damp and rosy on summer days, their puppy smell reminding me of Joe and Alex dashing in from school to drop their satchels and demand cold drinks. The overseas students were lonely and polite, chatting with me for a few minutes before going in to Heath. Some mature-age students were fulfilling a lifelong desire to learn music. Nervous and self-deprecating, as children never are, they were given five finger exercises and beginner's tunes. Before long Heath would have them progressing to *The Children's Bach* and Mozart's easy pieces. Their diligent efforts would echo in my garden studio, where perhaps I would be at a tricky point of a painting. Then I'd feel less frustrated, as though a magic circle surrounded us all, permitting our sincere efforts and elusive goals equal territory.

After one of Ruth's sittings, we made our way back to the house. It was a Friday and Heath was waiting to take me out to lunch.

'How's it going?' He sounded jovial.

'Very slowly.' Somehow this portrait was taxing me in ways I'd not run into before.

'My fault! I can't keep still,' Ruth suggested.

'Restless type?' Heath smiled at her. 'I know that feeling. What about joining us for lunch?'

'An excellent idea,' I agreed, for the time spent with Ruth always seemed too short. I looked forward to setting aside my working concentration and being together as friends.

As Ruth scrabbled in her scuffed handbag I realised she was looking for small change. I thought of my leather wallet, neatly packed with twenty-dollar notes. It was a relief when Heath spoke up.

'It's our shout.'

Ruth looked questioningly at us both, then smiled.

'That's really kind. Married couples don't ask me out as a rule.'

'Why's that?'

She shrugged. 'Two's company? I'm single. Maybe I'm a threat.'

I laughed. 'We'd love you to come.'

'Jolly good.' Heath was as pleased as I was.

There were several places we could eat out at the shopping centre. Don't ask me when that routine began. Heath did the banking on Fridays and I got in the habit of going along. We'd eat sandwiches at *The Coffeepot* or a Chinese lunch at *Lims*'.

Heath considered. 'Be nice to have a bottle of wine. What about the RSL?'

'Ruth wouldn't want to go to a club!'

'Why wouldn't I?'

'Smoke-ridden places, but the food's not bad,' Heath said.

'I could try the poker machines.'

I stared at her in surprise. I'd imagined us in some exclusive little restaurant. She wasn't the kind of person I associated with Bingo, meat raffles and gambling. But Heath was laughing.

'Australian culture it is! A bistro lunch and a five-dollar flutter.'

So it was to the club that we headed. In fact the atmosphere had improved since my last visit, many years before. The trestle tables had gone and the *smorgasbord* spread was fresh and appetising. Heath fetched red wine in glasses.

'Cask wine do?'

'I can't afford to support a palate,' Ruth said. She'd piled up her plate as though she hadn't had a proper feed in days.

Heath seemed thoughtful. 'What else do you do, Ruth, apart from having your portrait painted and drinking rough red?'

'I'm looking for a job.'

'What line of work?'

'Well, anything. The money from my book's completely dried up.'

'You could run a Creative Writing course,' I suggested. Teaching the rudiments of my own craft appealed to me. I'd offered my services to a couple of adult education colleges in case a vacancy came up. But she shook her head.

'I don't understand the process well enough.'

'Why not write another novel?'

'It's a funny game. I didn't plan the first one. I didn't expect to publish it. It was simply my story. I wanted to disown the parts about grief and cowardice and cruelty. And to acknowledge what was good. I just wrote it all down. It was an accident.'

'And you can't repeat your act?' Heath drained his glass as Ruth shrugged. 'Sounds like you've stopped living.'

'Heath!' I thought he sounded rude but Ruth wasn't put out.

'No-o-o. I wouldn't say so. Why, is that your own state of mind?'

Heath drained his glass. 'Well, life does become mundane.'

'I disagree. I want a century of new experience.'

'You'll pay!' Heath sniffed. 'Cheap red plays merry hell with my sinuses. But Ruth says What the hell! Anyone for a top-up?'

'Don't forget you're teaching this afternoon,' I reminded him. He was in a cheerful mood. He even patted my shoulder as he squeezed past with the empty glasses.

'Nobody takes me out to lunch and buys me wine,' Ruth said as we watched him walk over to the bar. She didn't sound envious, but wistful.

'I suppose I'm lucky.' Though it wasn't something I'd considered. Heath and I were a fixed pair, like Laurel and Hardy, Darby and Joan. We'd been like that forever, or so it seemed to me.

★　★　★

76

Ruth eased into our lives so subtly I could hardly remember a time when we weren't a threesome. Perhaps she filled the space between Heath and myself. I'm sure we served the same role in her life, for she had neither family nor citizenship to fall back on. Soon we were going everywhere together; to concerts, a picnic in King Edward Park, an art movie in town.

'Let's ask Ruth along to this.' Heath gave me a flyer advertising an exhibition by Elspeth Giotti, a local painter who went in for lumpy nudes.

'Oh, must we go? *Bacchus Rampant* . . . Imagine it!'

'Don't be so quick to judge. What's the harm in being seen at gallery openings if you're in the same game?' He meant that if I wasn't invited to exhibit often, I only had myself to blame. It was true that I avoided art gatherings and lived outside the friendships and cliques of the local art scene. When I was younger I'd sounded out that world, perhaps hoping to find a real sharing of the aims of painting. But I never did fit in. I stood on the fringes, not knowing what to say. I soon dropped out.

'I hate gallery openings. You know I do.'

'I'm sure Ruth would like to come along.' He knew her company would entice me. He was never out of place in a group. He'd spent his career in classrooms and staff rooms, giving lectures and master classes to interested audiences. My refusal to network was a mistake, he thought. 'Give her a ring and see if she's free,' he persisted. 'We'll ask the Scarfs along as well. We could take a run into Beaumont Street and eat Italian afterwards if Roly isn't too deeply in the red.'

He was smiling like a cherub. He could be charming and I knew he was trying to lift me out of my doldrums. Ruth's portrait was driving me to distraction. The features just refused to come together. I knew how moody I could be when work went badly so I laughed and gave in. It might be fun.

★   ★   ★

We met the Scarfs and Ruth outside the gallery. Rowena's latest pregnancy was well advanced and she looked tired. Hardly surprising, when she was in her forties. This would be child number seven. Roly really ought to call a halt to his breeding programme, I thought; though it took two to tango, obviously. For my friends, anyway, the sex urge was alive and well. One could sense that rapport between the pair. I'd never thought about it before. I just knew something had been lost between Heath and myself, though for days on end I might imagine we were just the same as ever. Then some sharp comment or sarcastic exchange would spring up out of nowhere, as though beneath our friendship and our routines some deep resentment simmered. Perhaps it showed.

'How are you, Barbs?' Rowena had a concerned expression as we walked up the stairs together. 'You look a bit down.'

'I'm fine! How are *you*, more to the point?'

'Normal. Swollen ankles, varicose veins, indigestion, peeing every half hour.' She laughed but I could tell the climb was a strain for her.

'You'll be pleased when the baby's born.'

'I guess.'

She sounded weary and I said no more.

Upstairs, I saw Elspeth Giotti, surrounded by an attentive group of admirers. I picked up a catalogue. The theme was supposed to draw some classical parallel with the Hunter wine-growing industry and the artist's massive canvases made me glad that Sophie had decided not to come along with us. Satyrs cavorted in murky groves; rearing erections sent families with children or old folk in tow scuttling away to the small still lifes of grapes and vine leaves hung inconspicuously in the far corner. The gallery was noisy, with a large crowd packed in. Adults juggled wine glasses and crumbling snacks. Children scampered about and did slides along the polished floor.

I waited at the far end of the gallery. The others had gone off — Heath and Ruth to collect champagne and Rowena to locate the toilet. Roly had joined the crowd. He loved social events and crowds. Like many teachers, he grizzled about his job but in fact he was a kid at heart; never happier than when he play-wrestled his boys, got a ball game going in the back yard or shouted orders to his wayward cats and dogs.

Ruth tracked me down and gave me a glass of champagne.

'What a bun fight! One well-dressed woman nearly trampled me. I expected her to snatch the glasses out of my hand.'

I took the hard-won trophy as Rowena waddled towards us.

'Here, take mine.' Ruth held out her glass. 'I'll get another one.'

'No thanks, I don't drink alcohol — the baby. Where's Roly? He'll find me some grape juice.'

'Should be plenty of that here, given the subject matter. What do you think of the show, Barbs?'

'To each his own.'

'The models must have had fun . . . Wonder how they kept it up?'

I sipped from my glass, feeling prudish. That was Roly's kind of humour, I'd have thought. As if he'd read my mind, he came towards us, leering.

'I say, you three! Better watch your backs, poised in a perilous place like that.'

We happened to be standing in front of a floor-to-ceiling exhibit where several ten-foot high satyrs bore down on playful maidens.

'Front or rear, nothing's scared!'

Ruth's innuendo surprised me. I moved away from their laughter. At a distance, the three of them were like a little band of wanderers about to step through the rococo frame and join the revels. I felt quite alone. When Heath came up and touched my arm, I stepped away from him.

'I saw you talking with Marcus Griffin,' I said. 'Isn't Marian here?'

'She's gone to some church congress. Just as well!'

I turned on a false smile. Once we'd have shared that view. Now I was like Marian; consigned to the people who went to church, did good deeds and avoided sexual allusions. I sipped the wine. Too dry, I decided; a fitting drink for me.

* * *

Rowena didn't want to go out afterwards for a meal.

'Spoilsport!' Roly said to her; reminding me how little he'd changed since we first met the Scarfs. He'd always had an insensitive streak and a few drinks didn't improve his nature. Poor Rowena looked worn out and I intervened.

'I'm tired too. Let's call it a day, but why not come over to dinner soon? I'll ask a few others and we'll make a night of it. Ruth, you'll come, won't you?'

'Love to.'

She'd left her car parked at our place. We all had a quick snack, then Heath persuaded her to stay and watch a piano recital on the ABC. He offered to lend her a video of *The Magic Flute* but she shook her head.

'You don't care for opera?'

'It's not that. I don't have a VCR.'

Often her throwaway comments reminded me how pinched her life must be. As she stood up to leave, I heard the front door slam and Sophie breezed in. She hovered shyly as I introduced her. I knew she was impressed that Ruth had been published. English was Sophie's best subject and at home she was often closeted away in her room, filling her diary or writing poetry.

'Pity she had to go home,' Sophie said as

Ruth's spluttering car pulled away.

'Never mind. We're having a dinner soon. You two can have a good chat then.'

'She wouldn't be interested in me.'

'Of course she would. Ruth's quite down to earth. Have you eaten yet?'

'We had pizza at Jenny's. Now I've got an assignment to finish.'

'Just make sure you tidy up your room tonight. Mrs. L. will be here first thing. You know what that means.'

'Oh no!'

I laughed as she went to salvage her treasures. Our home help was ruthless. Anything left lying would be sucked up into the vacuum cleaner or tossed into the bin. Heath and I were always up at the crack of dawn to precede Mrs. Looington. She was the perfect scape-goat to blame whenever anything went missing. Over the years we had managed to curb her to some extent. No longer did we discover entire rooms rear-ranged, Heath's computer disconnected, and my Guatemalan fertility pot turned to face the wall. She'd been coming to clean as long as we'd had Sophie. In a funny way, she was family.

★   ★   ★

It was just a week since Heath died. I was in bed when the doorbell shrilled. My thoughts flew to Ruth. Against all the odds, somehow I still hoped we could make up. But it was my home help who stood, feet planted on my *Welcome* doormat. She could convey complex messages with a stance. Her silence suggested that brooms and dusters could be a medium of sympathy if that was what I needed. On the other hand, she would leave if I preferred.

'I'd forgotten it's your day. I'm all at sea.'

'Not surprisun.' She trampled indecision underfoot, limping down the hallway. 'Bunion's killun me. How was the funeral?'

'A lot of Heath's relatives turned up.'

'Catholic service?'

'Yes. He accepted the Last Rites before he died.'

She nodded wisely. 'Insurance. Flowers have lasted well. Shop flowers are a shockun waste. Don't buy flowers for me, I tell my kids. Remind me of death. I'll grow me own thanks. Stuffy in here. I'll open up.'

She flung the windows open and frowned. 'Garden's gone to pot. Want me to send Neil over?'

She commanded an array of odd-jobbers to chop and deliver firewood, prune trees, paint or cart rubbish to the tip. She ran her own

84

domestic service for her married sons and their working wives. Those daughters-in-law might be thin, they might be pretty, but they knew nothun about cookun or cleanun. Lucky they had her to step in with her broom and casseroles. The girls weren't grateful. Always on some diet, they didn't eat cakes and biscuits or fried food. They'd waste away to sticks. Her own appetite was healthy. She made cottage pies by the batch, rissoles by the stack. She'd share them around, she'd fold the grandchildren's nappies and iron her sons' shirts until they told her to mind her own business.

She introduced me to assertiveness, though I'm sure she'd never heard the term. She believed in herself and in her own opinions. She knew exactly what was what, as she made free with views no liberal nineties woman could possibly get away with. How wonderful to be so free from ambivalence! She knew exactly how to deal with rapists, bludgers, immigrants. She had no interest in health trends. She was obese, she smoked, never in a month of Sundays would she be seen jogging or counting the calories in chocolate cheese-cake. *Lifestyle* was not a word in her vocabulary and the idea of *karma* would have made her laugh. Life was just a happening. You had the ups, you had the downs.

Ailments arrived mysteriously, like space debris. She had bronchitis, bunions, varicose veins, arthritis and high blood pressure. She produced these complaints like breaking stories, dramatically following up with a weather report that would herald one of her seasonal discomforts — prickly heat, the autumn sniffles, winter rheumatism and spring allergies. She swept them aside with her vigorous duster and mowed them down with her broom.

Today it was the bunion. The specialist wanted to excise it.

'We'll see about that!'

I wasn't in the mood to comment. She'd never taken any notice of my anti-smoking advice. Instead I sat down, and she looked at me with concern.

'You haven't had any breakfast, have you?'

I said I wasn't hungry. She ignored that, filling up the kettle and slapping bread into the toaster.

'Gotta keep up your strength.'

Under her watchful gaze, I forced down a slice of toast and carried my mug of tea into the bedroom. As a rule I washed and ironed while she did the cleaning, but today there was nothing much to do. One woman doesn't need household help. I thought it would be hard to justify keeping her on, even if I could afford it, but I knew I wasn't ready to face that issue. Of course we lived in different worlds. If we ever chanced to meet in a supermarket we would mention the specials and the weather, then stand awkwardly, waiting for the other to move on. Yet there was more to our relationship than mops and dusters. Once a week we trod some primordial female ground. Our efficiency used to frighten Heath, who would make himself scarce as though we might sweep him up and discard him in the Wiz-bin.

Left in peace, we'd gossip. Standing on the back steps, my basket of wet washing set down nearby, her cigarette fouling the fresh morning air, we'd talk. I could never match the stories she gathered on her rounds. Eagerly I followed the saga of the doctor's problems with their inground pool. I sympathised with the overworked lesbian lawyer whose girlfriend slept in late and expected the maid to pick up her dirty washing, and I approved when Mrs. L. resigned from this post, protesting not at the relationship but at its inequality. For her clientèle had better not make assumptions. She made it known she didn't need the small amount of cash.

She liked manners and money. She worked for professionals, artists, wealthy people, in order to share options different from her own. Recently she'd acquired a late-model car, not unlike Heath's, causing him to wonder how she could afford such a purchase. But in her heart I sensed she only toyed with luxury. She was most alive when talking about her family. She was the hub of complex relationships, as full of fights and feuds as they were of weddings, births and anniversaries. Her family tree spread its sheltering branches so far and wide it was impossible to imagine she'd ever be alone or lonely.

★　★　★

I hadn't much to say, that day.

'Should I keep comun?' she enquired as I handed her the usual notes. She was used to the shocks of death. Stillbirths, strokes, heart attacks and road accidents had assaulted her warm heart where I knew she kept a niche for Heath and myself.

She was waiting for my answer.

'Yes. Please. For the time being.'

Her nod acknowledged the future was too hard to think about. She stumped down the path. I saw her stop to inspect some blemish on the paintwork of the car. I wondered how many hours of housework that shiny duco represented. It mirrored some significance she didn't accord herself, for she spat on the hem of her dress and rubbed away the offending mark.

The house smelt unnaturally sweet and fresh, as it always did until daily living reasserted its homely odours. Would I ever feel like cooking meals to serve up to an empty table? I couldn't imagine it, any more than I could think about Heath clearly. I could summon up the image of my housekeeper, but my husband, the man I'd lived with all my married life, had vanished as though I'd never known him. I tried to grasp him in my mind. What kind of person was he? How had I thought of him as sensitive when he could say such hurtful things at times? Why had I accepted his financial control when he'd made such a mess of things? He'd always seemed popular and easy-going in company, yet all I could remember now were the lonely hours he spent by himself, his single bed abandoned. He'd had a moralistic streak that could make him seem immune from average human desires, yet he'd proved himself as weak as any man. Any man? Who was Heath and where was he now? His sandals by the back door were real, but my husband and life-long partner was a blank.

5

As I walked down to collect the mail, I noticed how weeds had run riot in the months of Heath's last battle. The borders had lost the cluttered charm of a cottage garden and become an overgrown tangle. Aphids and black spot smothered the rose bushes. The marguerites were a sprawl of brown flower heads and woody stems. Miniature shrubs had been choked by paspalum clumps. I could hardly believe this air of neglect had taken over in so short a time. We'd always shared the work, of course. Heath would be out at sunrise, watering and clipping, keeping an eye on seasonal pests; and I don't suppose I ever walked over to my studio without pausing to pull a few weeds. The garden was one interest we shared, even when we began to find it so hard to talk freely. Heath never did find it easy to show his feelings and, when the single beds arrived, up went that awful barrier between us.

Should one talk about these things? To express your feelings, to say what is right and what is wrong about your life, is to take an awful risk. You have to know yourself. You have to be quite sure of what you want. I was never that sort of person. Staring at the envelopes in my hand (bills, a charity appeal, one letter addressed to Mrs B. Barnes) I thought, without Heath, who is this woman?

The rates bill I stuck on the fridge door. The note was from Marian, saying I was welcome to visit the Griffins any time I liked. The images of the famine appeal were too horrible to consider and I crumpled the envelope unopened. Usually such mailings touched my heart but at present I had nothing to give.

The house was spotless, I had absolutely nothing to do and it wasn't even lunchtime. I kept imagining Heath returned from town, coming in the back door to share a cup of tea before we went off to our respective studios. When Helen phoned, offering to drive me to my yoga class, I said I didn't feel like going. She pressed me to come and have a meal at their place. Again I declined. Poor Helen! She did mean well. Why couldn't I get to first base with my daughter-in-law? Something about the bristles of her razor-cut and her muscular, toned look held my love at bay. I tried to compensate by saying how nice her house looked, how well the carpets had cleaned, how tasty her home-made muffins were. She'd glow with pleasure as though hungry for appreciation. I doubted that my reserved son paid her many compliments. Alex had his thriving practice and his modern home. He swam and played squash to keep fit. A good-looking man, my son. Helen went to the gym three times a week as well. She and Alex had such a tight grip on life. Theirs seemed to run like clockwork. One never heard of any of the dramas that continually swamped my home help as hubby was made redundant, a daughter-in-law had a breast lump, Craig did his back or the grandchild had a learning disorder. And yet I sensed something was wrong. Efficient she might be, but Helen wasn't happy.

I had no right to judge her. We'd all control existence if we could. Even Heath came back to his church at the end. Perhaps the rituals of prayer and anointing gave him some sense of direction as he faced the unknown. As a teacher, he was systematic and methodical. Though he was an excellent pianist, he rarely displayed the true performer's risk-taking dynamism. I was the disorderly partner . . . always accommodating and easily influenced. Fortunately I hadn't grown up in the era of teenage rebellion, or I might have tried drugs and alcohol to keep up with my peers. As it was, I met Heath and drifted into marriage. I expected him to make the decisions. He was the man.

Joe's irresponsible life has given me a glimpse of how I might have been. Joe drove Heath to distraction but I could make sense of my boy's wildness. Morality hadn't been drummed in to me, as it had to Heath. My parents were average Anglicans who sent me to a state school. Nothing in my childhood placed me among a select minority like Heath and Ruth. She was a Jew; Heath a Catholic. These were stamps that moulded their very cores. They were both conscience-ridden rebels who justified their own behaviour, as though guilt and persecution allowed them leeway. While I was just like my friend, Rowena Scarf. We let others define us as they wanted us to be. Keeping the peace, I called it. I was middle-aged before I realised how weak I was. Then I went too far. Really, why did I take that arbitrary stand on sex? From that point, everything went wrong.

Heath and I were at loggerheads; each in need of something to fill the empty space between us. And it was just around that time that Ruth came into our lives. She was naturally on the guest list Heath and I had put together for our dinner party, along with the Scarfs, the Griffins, and Alex and Helen. As I was preparing the entrées, Joe turned up out of the blue.

'How's my favourite mum?' He grinned and swept me off my feet in his bear hug.

'Put me down! Why didn't you ring and say you were coming?'

'Spur of the moment trip. I've brought Ans; my new lady. Where's Soph?'

'At school, of course. Your father's out too. Bring Ans inside.'

'Later, OK? She wants to get over to her sister's place and drop off our gear.'

'So you're staying there?'

He nodded. Well, we both knew what Heath thought about Joe's string of girl-friends. Women friends, these days. My older son was looking a little seedy; boots down at heel, jeans scruffy. The corn silk hair of childhood was a dirty blonde, touched with grey. He wasn't far off forty.

'Soph doing OK?'

'Very good at music, and a reasonable student. She'd do better if she studied more.'

'Chip off the old block?'

I smiled. He'd been an unruly boy, never academic; a worry to us in adolescence as much as his brother had been a source of pride. Of course Heath had every right to remind me Joe was irresponsible. Weren't we bringing up his daughter? For all that, Joe's optimism never failed to cheer me up. Nothing could stop him in his tracks for long.

'Reckon she'd like to go out with us tonight?'

'Better if you come here.' I spoke firmly, not wanting Sophie to be confronted with yet another of his lady friends. 'You've timed things well. We're having a few friends over to dinner. You can see your father and Alex.' I felt a wistful hope that we could be a family again. Sometimes we all seemed like indifferent strangers.

'Cool, if Ans can come. Come out and say hello.' He hesitated. 'Mum, lend me twenty bucks? I'm strapped for cash and the car needs gas.'

I nodded and went to get my purse. That's how it was between us. Affection, flattery, sometimes a transaction I kept quiet about. I knew I indulged Joe. Somehow you couldn't do favours for Heath or Alex. With Joe, it was a matter of accommodate or lose him. I'd had to forgive plenty of his mistakes. Oddly enough, when the shock or anger faded, they'd deepened my affection for him. He didn't make demands. There'd be no problem if I said no. I sensed he'd help me out, if I ever became the needy one. So our relationship cost me a little money and a diplomatic silence where Heath was concerned. He thought Joe was a sponger. But the world runs on transactions and, amid those myriad deals, I thought money was an honest need and the easiest part of oneself to share.

'Here. An advance birthday present.' I gave him the spare fifty I kept hidden in my purse. 'Now, how about introducing me to Ans?'

'We've been shacked up since Christmas. Neat chick. She's got a little girl.'

His vocabulary was taking on the outmoded style of his clothes but he swaggered just the same as we walked outside, where his fair-haired passenger sat waiting. She saw us and stepped out of the car. I thought she looked pleasant and self-possessed; not Joe's usual flashy type, which was more than I could say for the vehicle.

'I'm Joe's mother. Hi!'

Joe gave the bonnet of the old Valiant a loving pat. 'What do you reckon? She's a beauty, heaps of grunt. I'll put fats and a spoiler on her one day when I'm cashed up.'

We stood there exchanging pleasantries before they took off with much revving and a squeal of tyres. I wondered what Heath would say when they arrived at our carefully planned dinner party. Sophie would be excited. She hardly knew her father. The photo she kept of him was an old one, staged for publicity back when Joe had a musical career. He'd played guitar around the clubs and pubs. Youth and music — a heady mix. His smile, his pose proclaimed *Look out, world; here I come!* Well, every young girl needed a hero and Sophie's might as well be Joe, as long as she could sustain the illusion.

★   ★   ★

Sophie was noncommittal when I told her Joe and Ans were coming to dinner. She went through phases of writing to him, then waiting in vain for some response. It did no good, explaining that her father simply wasn't the letter-writing kind. Now she seemed more excited about meeting Ruth.

'Should I pretend I've read her book, Nan?'

I laughed at her worried expression.

'She'll think I'm dumb.'

'She'll think you're very nice. Just be yourself.'

'I don't know what to wear.'

'Nothing fancy — it's informal.'

She took an hour to dress. When she emerged, carrying pages covered in her schoolgirl's writing, she was draped in black from head to toe, a pair of round-rimmed glasses she'd not used for several years perched on her nose. I could imagine her in some fifties basement filled with smoke haze and the wails of avant-garde jazz.

'No makeup?'

'You said not to make a fuss. Nan, would it be rude if I asked Ruth to look at one of my creative writing stories?'

'Why not?'

'My English teacher hasn't got a clue. Listen to what she wrote on this. *Verbs please! One adjective, not four! You over-write but good effort, B+*. Overwrite, when she teaches Shakespeare! 'O treble woe fall ten times treble on that cursed head . . . ' What are the mushrooms for?'

'Beef Stroganoff.'

'Why take the stalks off? Rowena uses them.'

'Some do, some don't. My mother taught me this way.'

'Then I suppose that's what I'll do, when I'm a cook. Can I help?'

'You could start making the salad. They'll be here soon.'

We worked companionably in the small kitchen. Sophie never made me feel I was only a substitute parent. Her mother left her so young, poor waif that she was. I can still see her after Joe brought her to us after one of his band tours. He'd tried, but that was no life for a little girl; traipsing the countryside, no routine, strange hotels and takeaways. Her underwear was ragged and there were holes in her shoes. What choice did I have? I'd never regretted having Sophie. But I was never asked. It was one of those roles I stepped into, wearing my virtuous smile, pretending there was no burden in it for me.

I was busy with the entrées when the first guest rang the doorbell.

'There's your author.' I knew it must be Ruth. The Scarfs were notoriously late and Joe would come straight in. Waving an anxious signal, Heath dashed through the kitchen, a bath towel round his waist. 'Ask her in, Sophie, and offer her a drink.'

'I can't. Vanessa isn't here.'

Embarrassments sprout like pimples when one is only fifteen. 'The Scarfs will be here soon. Now go!' And I gave her a sympathetic push.

However, by the time the Scarfs and the Griffins arrived, Sophie and Ruth were chatting like old friends. Sophie introduced Vanessa as her best friend. Rowena, pregnant and sway-backed in her loose white *broderie anglaise* frock, sat down with a weary sigh. Roly and Marcus, both teachers, were soon talking shop. I left Heath to hand round the drinks and went back to the kitchen. Alex, who said he'd been delayed at the clinic, arrived next with Helen.

'I made this, Mum.' She set down an

elaborate confection in a crystal bowl.

'It looks wonderful. What is it?'

'Rum Baba. It should go in the fridge.'

'Good idea. Come and meet the others. Alex, you'll never guess who's coming.'

My son seemed indifferent when I told him Joe was in town. All the same, I had high hopes for the night. To sit down at table with my husband and my two boys was a joy I hadn't experienced for a long time. Perhaps old rifts would be forgotten. Instead of resenting and judging one another, we might rediscover the family love we used to feel.

'Alex, open these bottles for me?' I handed him the Scarfs' Shiraz, and Chablis from the Griffins. Expertly he drew the corks and took the bottles to the other room. Behind us, the girls were quietly dipping in to the various pre-dinner snacks. 'How about you two young ladies pass the nibbles round?'

They went off, laden with savouries, canapés and dips. Helen, who was assessing the company from the kitchen door, turned to me.

'Is that your friend Rowena? The woman in the white frock?'

I nodded. I suppose I often mentioned Rowena; we were such longterm friends.

'I'm surprised she'd risk having a baby at her age.'

'She's an old hand — it's her seventh,' I said lightly, though I must admit Rowena was looking very tired.

'Seven!'

Helen was horrified. I guessed a baby wasn't on her want list. I couldn't imagine a toddler in that spotless house. Yet my instincts made me babble on.

'Children bring unexpected joy, you know. Oh, there's the work and the expense, but a baby taps in to wells of love you never knew existed . . . '

I stopped, realising I had said far too much. For a moment, Helen's face seemed to crumple and I imagined I saw tears in her eyes. Then an angry flush replaced the look of sorrow.

'Please mind your own business and don't lecture me on what's good for me!'

'I wasn't . . . I'm sorry, Helen.' But she had stalked out. Whatever nerve I'd touched was raw but I had no time to think about it as Joe and Ans arrived just then and we were swept up in a further round of introductions.

'Your husband's lucky, getting that appointment in the States.' Roly, seated beside Marian, sounded envious.

'It will be interesting,' Marian acknowledged. 'I'm hoping we can make a stop-over on the way. I've always wanted to visit the

Holy Land.' She spoke to Ruth. 'The idea of seeing Bethlehem and Nazareth, and standing on the Mount of Olives, really thrills me.'

'Don't miss Jerusalem,' said Ruth. 'It's a wonderful city. Living history.'

'Oh, I can imagine! Do you follow the Jewish faith?'

'Not as a religion. My parents were agnostics.'

'I thought all Jews followed the Old Testament,' said Marian.

'Like Christians, we vary! I'm afraid religious fanatics did us a lot of damage. By the time Romans, Crusaders and Muslims had finished with us, we were scattered all over the place. Well, at last we're back on our own land.'

'At some cost!' Alex jumped in to the conversation feet-first. 'The Palestinians would probably prefer to have their homes and farms returned.'

'Those terrorists! They use Allah as their excuse to attack us and murder us.'

I hoped the evening wasn't going to veer off into a religious argument.

'The glasses could do with a refill,' I suggested. 'What will you have, Rowena?'

'Nothing alcoholic, thanks.'

'Heath, there's fresh orange juice in the fridge.'

'Of course, my dear. My wife, the master of ceremonies!' He made a mock salute and left the room. These snide little digs were becoming a habit with him. I felt miserably alone. Ruth turned the conversation elsewhere.

'How long to go, Rowena?'

'A few months.' She sighed.

'They can seem interminable, as I remember it.'

'I keep telling myself it won't be long. I had a scan recently. It's a little girl.'

I glanced at Helen, who sat stiffly, her face pale and mask-like.

'I always wanted a daughter. My only son, Asher, is in the army.'

'You must worry about him.'

'We're used to it. Everybody has to serve. After the call-up period, most people stay part-time reserves.'

Alex was back to his stirring. 'That recent footage on the Golan Heights looked nasty. Would he have been involved?'

Ruth shrugged. 'Permanent army would have been called out before the reserves. Asher's trying to get out. He's served his time and he's a very sensitive boy.'

'Must be hard for him, shooting civilians.'

'Alex!' I would have kicked him under the table if we'd been seated there. 'Dinner's ready, everyone. Please sit down and I'll bring in the starters.' In the kitchen I glared at Heath. 'Could you possibly keep your sarcasm for our private life? This evening is becoming a disaster.' He saw I meant business. By the time I was ready to set out the entrées, people were seated at table and the conversation was apparently safely set on Israel's weather.

'Very hot and dry in August,' Ruth was saying as she nodded appreciatively at the fresh fruit compote. 'October, thunderstorms. Snow on the hills in January. Spring's lovely. Wildflowers everywhere, and the scent of crushed rosemary underfoot.'

'Could we go then, Marcus?' Marian suggested.

'The PLO might be taking pot-shots at the tourists.'

Alex seemed determined to be argumentative but Ruth began to laugh. She sounded almost flirtatious as she took him up.

'You're a real stirrer! You remind me of Asher, though you're old enough to know better. He's good-looking, like you, too. What do you do for a living?'

'I'm a chiropractor.'

'I must pay you a visit. I have back problems from my own army days. Oh yes, the girls are called up too, at eighteen. I soon learned how to strip down a gun and put it back together again. Luckily, I never had to fire at a human target. Women were mainly drivers or radio operators.'

Alex was eyeing her with muted respect now. Her tone changed. She sounded maternal as she spoke to him as though they were the only people present.

'You know, Alex, if you'd been a little boy in Tel Aviv when the War of Independence started, you'd have spent your childhood dodging bullets. During the siege of Jerusalem, you'd have gone hungry and thirsty and you might have lost your parents or your brother. We're products of our environment, you see. How is it you don't pursue the arts, the way Heath and Barbie do?'

'I decided to make money.' But as he returned her gaze I noticed his smile was warm enough, and he'd lost interest in provoking her.

As we progressed to the main course, I hoped Joe and Ans didn't feel too out of place among this group of professionals and high-income earners. *Can someone shove those buns along?* had been Joe's sole contribution to the talk so far, but at least he looked as though he was enjoying the meal. Marian was not going to drop her chance to question a local first-hand, and went on plying Ruth with questions that she answered good-naturedly while her dinner cooled. One couldn't mistake the affection with which she spoke of the brilliant blue Mediterranean, the yellow coastal dunes and cool green hills, and the blood-red poppies covering the fields in April.

'Forget Tel Aviv, Marian. Jerusalem is the world's second-oldest inhabited city. You have to see the glow of its stone buildings.'

'Of course!' Marian sounded reverent. '*Jerusalem the Golden.*'

'From the airport you drive through young forests and hills terraced with old vineyards and olive groves. Of course the city's on a hill. You can look down on the Old City, with its two miles of walls, twelve metres high.'

'Is one allowed in?'

'Oh yes, they took down the barbed-wire barriers after the '67 war. There's still four quarters; Christian, Muslim, Armenian and Jewish, and you can take your pick of churches, synagogues, mosques . . . ' She broke off, smiling. 'I'm sounding like a travelogue! Won't someone else please monopolise the conversation?'

'But it's fascinating! Marcus, we simply have to make a stop there. I'm surprised you could ever bear to leave, Ruth. Will you go back one day?'

'Oh no. I doubt that. I've made my choice. My dream is that Asher will join me here one day. Now Roly, you were saying that you teach?'

'School masters don't teach, my dear, we force-feed conscripts. You keep on entertaining us with your intelligent observations — what man could ask for more?'

Roly was well into the wine by the sound of him. Really, I wondered how Rowena put up with him sometimes.

Suddenly my friend came to life. Hearing education mentioned, she dropped the abstracted look of late pregnancy. 'We follow Rudolf Steiner's philosophy of learning, Ruth. Have you read him?' Ruth shook her head. 'It's just so important to offer education at the teachable moment.'

Their older children had transferred to the State system but I knew the younger Scarfs' education entailed considerable expense. At their house, overdue bills bristled under the fridge magnets, they had no TV or video, and their furniture had that look of shabbiness one associates with old holiday cottages and summers beside the beach.

'Children need the hands-on stuff,' Roly said, refilling his glass. 'Everyone's technology crazy these days. Kids need to grow things, make clothes, build furniture.'

'Surely in this day and age science and computer studies are essential?' Helen ventured.

'At six and seven, no way!'

'Maths and science should come later.' Rowena firmly set down her knife and fork to make her stand. 'Music is our earliest language. Steiner thinks of the music of the spheres as a universal energy we rest in. Am I putting it right, Roly?'

'This is too mystical for me,' Heath protested. 'Give me crotchets and quavers and plenty of practice. Anyway, what's wrong with technology? If an old bird like me can deal with computers, why shouldn't the young ones?'

'Well, Steiner said one mustn't force a young child's mind. I can lend you his books if you like.'

Joe spoke up loudly. 'Ans sends Hedda to the Bingara local primary school. Somehow she's figured out how to read and do arithmetic. Hey, she must be a genius.'

Heads swivelled and the conversation came to an abrupt halt as everyone stared. Ans took a sip of Chablis and then left the glass untouched. At least she had changed into a blouse and skirt. Joe looked so out of place in his faded jeans and half-buttoned shirt. My boy knew just how to draw negative attention his way. He grinned and tucked in to his food while Rowena, trying to smooth over the atmosphere, asked, 'You have a little girl, Ans? How old is she?'

'She's seven and quite bright. I'm sure as mothers we only want to do the best for our children.' Her good-natured smile immediately promoted her in my estimation.

Marian nodded warmly. 'How true! We all do our best. And what's your line of work, Joe?'

'Dad's a musician.' Sophie smiled proudly as she spoke.

Joe shrugged. 'There's not much work around in the music industry now. In the 80s we toured Noumea and New Caledonia.'

'I've got that photo, Dad! What was it like, touring?'

'Hot and sticky. Spiders big as birds, living in the telegraph wires. French cooking and lots of girls.'

'Sounds a bit old-hat.' Alex chipped in. 'Got a job now?'

'Do a bit on the land.'

'You're farming?'

'Could say that. Not a bad living either, so long as they don't legalise the crop.'

Vanessa and Sophie giggled but Heath's lips were compressed. Trust Joe!

'Got any beer, Dad? Ans and I don't like this fancy stuff.'

I pushed back my chair. 'In the fridge,' I said. 'Come out with me and get it.'

Silently Joe followed me and rummaged for the beer.

'Must you upset your father like that? You know what he thinks about drugs.'

'Mum, I'm not a pusher. We smoke a few joints, that's all, like half the rest of the population do.'

'I don't want to know. Don't embarrass your daughter, that's all.'

'Soph's growing up fast. I'd like to be a better dad to her.'

'If you mean that, I wouldn't put it off. She'll be an adult in a few years.'

He nodded. His face was scored with deep lines from too many late nights spent in smoky clubs and pubs. Most of the sharp lads in their spangled suits would have abandoned their dreams. The few who clung on would have to scrounge for work, entertaining an ageing audience who sought nostalgia.

★ ★ ★

When everyone had gone home, Heath helped clear up. Scowling, he dumped plates on the sink.

'You'd like to think your children were your friends.'

Heath had hardly been on friendly terms with his own parents but I didn't remind him of that. 'Don't mind Joe. He was just feeling odd man out.'

'What's new? No reason to broadcast his seedy lifestyle among my friends.'

'Our friends. They can see the situation.'

'Anyone with two eyes can see the situation. Joe's a bum.'

'Don't say that, Heath!' His harshness upset me. I loved both my boys. I wished he could see past Joe's provocation to the rough-and-ready affection in his nature. Heath hadn't been a lavish father. If I suggested the boys could do with a bit more pocket money, he used to disagree. *Let them get a paper run and learn the value of money.* Alex had got the message but Joe had tried to bully us. He took a childish, almost aggressive delight in confirming his father's worst opinion of him. In a world like Ruth's he probably had the makings of a terrorist.

'You always make excuses for him,' Heath grumbled.

'You always put him down!'

'He's totally irresponsible. Who raised his daughter? How much has he contributed to Sophie's upkeep over the years?'

'Heath!' My warning came too late. Sophie, arriving with a load of dishes, stood stock still in the doorway. Her hurt face was devastating. Without a word she put down the plates and walked out.

'She'll imagine she's a financial burden to us now.'

'Rubbish! She knows better than that.'

But I didn't think so. Heath had never been dependent. Until I took my stand, he'd never had any idea how a beggar feels.

6

Plans for the future were more than I could manage. Each morning I nibbled a token breakfast, made lists of tasks I would have to attend to eventually, then sat waiting for the mail. On my way to the letterbox I made mental notes of jobs to be done in the garden, which day by day seemed more like a wilderness. My heart would race as I reached in for the letters, although I could not say what I was waiting for. It was madness to imagine Ruth would try to break the silence I had so clearly established between us. I carried the day's mail inside, scanned its dreary contents, then sat with my cup of cooling coffee, lost in memories of the past.

That dinner party, for example. Looking back, why hadn't I understood we were jungle creatures, separate and secretive? The seeds of all that followed were already sown as we ate and drank and chatted our way through that comfortable suburban get-together. I remembered the way Heath kept up appearances as gracious host, saving his anger until the guests went home.

So, at the table, we adults decorously

enjoyed Helen's Rum Baba and fresh peaches. Side by side in the papasan chair, the girls ate their fruit, dripping juice and licking their fingers. Afterwards, the men drifted aside, talking about work. Marian, Helen and Ans seemed to be at ease in a group while Ruth was alone, observing. Sophie went to sit with Joe and I watched him wind strands of her dark hair around his finger as he talked; her soft gaze forgiving all his neglect of her. I overheard him telling her stories of his long-ago tour.

'We were playing at the good old *Spectac* . . . Tahitian drumming, dancing, *Tahiti's Queen of Song* act. The fire swallower was a card. Once he set his hair on fire. Gee you'd have laughed! I'll give you a demo. Got any matches and a piece of paper?'

As Joe was stuffing a flare of paper into his mouth, Heath walked over from his group. 'We don't need any pyromania tonight, thanks.' Joe crumpled the charred remains and dropped them on the carpet while Sophie's giggle sounded nervous. Just then Roly, who'd also come to see what was going on, picked up some after-dinner mints. He tossed one to Vanessa then turned to Sophie.

'Sweets for the sweet?'

She smiled up at him and opened her

mouth compliantly. Her expression was contented as she rested her head against Joe and I felt a warning pang on her behalf. The willing lines of her body suggested a need that might be taken advantage of.

I wasn't sorry when the party broke up. Rowena made the first move and Roly, on the quiet, told me she was showing toxic signs. He was evidently feeling the strain of their unplanned pregnancy as well.

'Tell me if you need any help,' I reminded him. We sometimes acted as their confidantes. Once they went home, others soon followed.

Ans thanked me for inviting her.

'How long have you been with Joe?' I wondered.

'A year, give or take. So far it's working out.'

'Why Bingara? It must be a very small community.'

'Country life suits us. One roof's much like another.'

I liked her frankness. 'Does Joe plan to take Sophie out before you leave?' I could hardly ask her to let them go alone but she seemed to understand.

'I'm sure he will. They should have some private time.'

It seemed Joe was finally with a non-possessive and nice young woman. That was a relief, although I guessed Heath was going to make a fuss and I felt disappointed that Alex and Joe had hardly exchanged two words all evening.

Ruth was the last to leave. She seemed to read my mind as she thanked me for inviting her.

'Your sons have very different natures.'

'We mothers have to accept them as individuals; and they all leave in the end.'

'Asher's never left me, never in his heart.'

I found her remark strange. Her son was a soldier, far away in a foreign land.

'Hasn't he married? Surely some pretty girl will whisk him off?'

Instead of laughing, Ruth sounded adamant. 'He won't get caught like that. We made a vow we'd always be together one day — when he gets out of the army.'

Perhaps dutiful sons did exist. To me, her words rang strangely, as though she'd drawn aside a garment and shown me an unhealthy growth. But the mood changed in a flash as Heath joined us.

'We were discussing our children,' Ruth said.

'Barbie blinkered as ever behind her rose-coloured spectacles, I suppose?'

I was tired of his needling. He seemed to feel company made it safe to make fun of me.

'At least I don't demand proof of everything, the way you do.'

Ruth seemed amused. 'Is that right, Heath? Prove a seed will become a flower? Explain electricity? Love?'

'I have no problem with flowers and light globes. Effects speak for themselves.'

'And love?'

'Ah, that's the tricky one.'

'240 volts where you least expect it!'

I was glad when Heath laughed; in a better mood, perhaps he'd shorten the forthcoming lecture I knew awaited me when everyone had gone.

However, lying in my single bed that night, I decided the evening hadn't gone so badly. Heath was over his outburst and slept peacefully enough across the room. I forgot Helen's brusqueness, Roly's flirting, Ruth's strange attitude about her son. In my mind I composed a Dégas-type tableau. Background figures, Alex, Helen and Ans relaxed beside the Griffins on the long sofa. Ruth and Heath stood nearby, inclined towards each other in an attitude of banter. Rowena sat in the shadows, calm hands resting on the tight mound of her baby. Radiant in a high value shaft of light, the two girls reclined lazily in a papasan chair, Vanessa's thick fair hair tumbling to her shoulders and Sophie's mouth moist with peach juice. Roly's full red lips were smiling as he watched them. I would make a sketch in the morning. One day I might want to paint that scene.

★ ★ ★

All creativity seemed to have deserted me since Heath's illness struck. I couldn't bring myself to go near my studio. Even walking outside in the garden was painful. Heath had laid the path himself, brick by brick. Together we'd chosen the ground covers and rockery plants, working side by side as we tucked them into crevices between the stones. Hard to visualise how bare the soil was a few years ago. The whole yard had lost its claim to be a garden and had taken on an air of desolation. Perhaps I was no more than a tenant here. The house would have to be sold. I would have to deal with things soon. Soon. I kept repeating that word. The state of my finances was another issue I simply couldn't face. Alex and Helen were doing the worrying on my account. Alex offered me a loan. There was talk of building on a granny flat. But I couldn't see myself living there. There was simply too much tension between them.

The problem was Helen's parents. At first I thought Alex was being selfish when he complained about the drain on Helen's time and energy but, as he talked, I had to acknowledge his point. Anxious neighbours had called him out when the poor old father went wandering after dark, half-naked and confused.

'Now her mother thinks she's being poisoned. She won't eat unless Helen cooks the food in front of her.' It wasn't like my son to open up to me. 'Helen's over there for hours every day. It's just too much.'

'It does sound so.'

'Mother? Please have a talk with her?'

'I don't want to interfere.'

'I can't get through to her. She insists it's her duty.'

'This kind of degeneration only gets worse, Alex. Perhaps time will help her see they need professional care?'

'Try telling Helen that. She has a bad case of Catholic conscience.'

His words jolted me uncomfortably into the past. I used to disparage Heath like that. I'd forgotten Helen was brought up as a Catholic. She didn't go to church but there'd been a fuss about it at the time they married.

'Perhaps she was very religious as a girl? Why did she leave the church, do you know?'

'Something happened. She felt let down.' Alex sounded reflective. 'I never understood that RC stuff with Dad. I mean, he didn't believe in it, but he was so judging, you know?'

I didn't want to talk about it. It didn't seem right. Heath was dead. Perhaps I should have tried harder to understand him. 'Have you really tried to talk about this with Helen?'

'It only makes her angry. We end up fighting.'

I felt sorry for him. He sounded so confused. 'Would she talk to me about her parents?'

'It's worth a try.' He managed to smile at me.

★ ★ ★

But when I did broach the subject, diplomatically, I saw what he meant.

'How are your parents, Helen?' We were washing up after an excellent roast dinner. At once she began to spill out details of their many problems.

'Dad's wandering. Mum's quite paranoid. I'm afraid it's become worse recently. You'd have to understand their war experiences. They were only kids then. Now it's all come back to haunt them. I'm the only one they trust.'

'That's quite a responsibility on your

shoulders. Might it be time to look into professional care for them?'

But at once she flared up. 'How heartless do you think I am? They never abandoned me.'

'Surely you could visit them, every day if necessary.'

She scrubbed the baking dish in silence. My words didn't deserve a reply. It was a matter they would have to sort out for themselves.

* * *

The following week I forced myself to phone a real estate agent. He carried out an inspection, admired the position and presentation of my home and assured me he could sell the place quickly provided I made arrangements to tidy up the grounds.

'When my husband was alive we were both keen gardeners.' I needed him to understand that the present unkempt state was not my normal attitude. 'This jungle appeared while he was ill. That took all our time, you see. The hospital. Visiting. All the different treatments.'

'Very difficult for you. Very sad. You're wise to sell up. Too many memories. Start afresh. Many people do. Would you like me to list the property now?'

'Oh no.' I felt gripped by anxiety. 'Not immediately. I'm just getting an idea.'

'This is a good time of year to sell. Plenty of enquiries at the office.'

'I'll get back to you. I must arrange a gardener. I would have to think where to move to.'

'If you want to delay the move, I know of a very nice retirement complex planned nearby. They've already started work.'

'I don't think I'm ready for the old folks' home just yet!' The whole exercise seemed more and more like a dream to me. Heath wasn't dead. At any minute he'd swing the car into the driveway. *I'm home, Barbie, put the kettle on?*

We'd get to work on the weeds, we'd prune, we'd cut back and plant and soon our garden would be a safe and restful haven again.

'These days, people like to move down to a smaller living space. Less work, more time for relaxation. I can show you through the units when they're built.'

I supposed he hoped for a double sale. He was a businessman. Why would he care that a widow in her fifties might still visualise some life for herself? I accepted his engraved card and watched with relief as he drove away in his late-model car.

Unreality persisted as I telephoned Welfare enquiries. Some young thing seemed to think I should apply for Job Search allowance, although I explained I had never been employed in my entire life. I remembered Ruth telling me how hard it was, getting work at her age. I was ten years older. Somewhere between youth and old age I was adrift in a world presenting me with job expectations, granny flats and retirement villages. How was I supposed to deal with it all? Denial would do. I still had my little nest egg and, if bills came, I simply wouldn't open them. Charity appeals could go in the bin. I'd be one of the needy soon enough. A displaced person, I'd be expected to move along without a fuss.

* * *

Mrs. Looington refused to indulge me. The next time she came, she frowned at my dressing gown. 'Sick?' She sounded disbelieving. In the living room, she whipped up the blinds. 'The place for dead flowers is in the rubbish.' She whisked them away and collected up the display of sympathy cards.

'I haven't answered those yet.'

'What for? You're not swoppun Christmas cards. Have you packed up hubby's clothes?'

I shook my head.

123

'Get rid'uvum. No use hangun on to things. Only upsets you. A woman I worked for, her son got killed. She never changed a thing in eight years. Kept his room the same, wouldn't even let me run the vacuum round. That room's stayun like it is, she said. What happened? She had a breakdown.'

'I can't seem to get motivated.'

'You gettun outa the house? You can't sit about sad and sorry.'

'I have plenty to do. Sort Heath's clothes. I should contact a few of his pupils.'

'You be sellun the pianner?'

The idea of someone else owning Heath's piano shocked me. 'Sophie will need it, when she comes back from Bingara.'

'That's if she does. I'll start the dustun.'

The house was noisy with the past that day. Unmusical runs issued from the piano as Mrs. L. swooped with her vigorous duster. The windchimes clanked in the garden and ghosts rattled the hangers in the wardrobe as I took out Heath's clothes and draped them in a pile. I emptied the drawers of his underwear and socks. I lined up his worn shoes in pairs. I sat and picked pillballs from his woollen sweaters and cried over these records of our long years together. How strange it was to go through his pockets like a thief. I was a grave robber, reburying Heath who had nothing useful to offer me. Mrs. L. helped pack his things in cardboard boxes.

'The Sallies will find a home for these.'

Of course she was right. I was glad as we carried the boxes out to her car. It would be a relief to open the wardrobe and see only my own skirts and jackets hanging there. She ordered me to start going for a walk every morning. Meekly I agreed.

Once I was out of the house, my repetitive thoughts grew calm. I could imagine I was in the country as I walked towards the mountain at the top of our street. Magpies and currawongs swooped above thistled paddocks where cattle browsed. Beyond that open grassland, **No Entry** gates demarcated the quarry. Petitions went round from time to time but I couldn't see much would come of objecting when the quarry had been there longer than we had. I was used to the muffled echoes of explosives and the occasional ground tremors like distant earthquakes.

I'd never walked up this far before. Now I saw how the mountainside was wounded. Remaining tiers of bush clung sparsely to the rock face. Faced by chained gates, I turned and made my way downhill, passing trim gardens, drowsy cats and watchdogs baying at the fence lines. The early morning brought me into contact with a new clan — joggers, power walkers, and dogs with their leashed owners amusingly in tow. The lake winked its blue eye between suburban roofs.

Not far from home a big building project was in progress. I scanned the heritage-lettered sign. *Banksia Grove. Superior Retirement Villas for the Over-55s.* Not a banksia in sight. Like a war zone, churned clay was toothed with bulldozer tracks and studded with the oozing stumps of several grand old eucalypts. Severed trunks and limbs lay in stacks, awaiting removal. Deliveries of stones, roof tiles, bricks and timber were dumped about on the razed ground. The earth was scooped down to bedrock. What plants could ever flourish on that mean foundation? Remembering the endless loads of peat moss, manure and hay that Heath had lugged from the nursery to build up our soil, I felt guilty to have let things go so badly at home. I owed it to him to stop feeling sorry for myself. I wouldn't employ some unimaginative handyman who would reduce our garden to razed suburban order. I would do the work myself. Yes, a little each day, until I had put things back they way we'd made them. The thought cheered me. I stepped up my pace and headed home. Mrs. L. was right. I did feel better for the outing. At the gate I viewed the garden with new determination. I had a project.

There was a card from Ruth in the mail. Not one of those well-meaning sympathy messages that somehow look so depressing — just a pressed flower in a fold of paper, and a few words scrawled in her jagged handwriting.

What can I say? Thinking of you, Love, Ruth.

I stood there in the weak spring sunshine, reading the words over and over. During the months of Heath's illness, I'd cut off contact with her and dismissed her from my life. But I doubted a day had passed since then when I hadn't thought of her and wondered if I'd been fair. Our lives were in turmoil. I had to ask myself what part I'd played in those events. I'd thought of writing her a letter but felt unsure. I hoped she might make the first move. Since her own devastating news, she must be more isolated than ever. Surely she must miss our friendship? Now here was the proof of that.

Slowly, as I had come to know her, I realised that whatever social contacts she'd had in Israel, here in Australia she was Ruth amid the alien corn. Nobody cared that a gifted writer lived quietly in our city. Other names occupied the literary headlines; other books held space in the review columns. She was passé, broke and available to step into the space that had grown between Heath and myself. She came between the bad habits we'd slipped into. I didn't nag and chivvy him and he didn't mention his ailments when she was around. Ruth was a challenge to Heath. They liked to spar on political or social issues and she showed him his preconceptions. He had to realise a woman could survive alone. She never spoke of a partner or husband. About the sexual encounters I remembered in her book, and there were several, nothing lasting was implied.

I was curious about that. Casually, while she sat posed, I'd try to fill in her hazy background.

'Were you married, back in Israel?'

She answered me obliquely. 'Asher's still there. It's five years since I saw him.' She sounded almost desolate. I suppose she had no one else. I could understand loneliness but I wanted to warn her all mothers must step back or become the butt of jokes about possession. Yet what right had I to offer unsought advice?

'You've moved,' I said. 'Can you turn your head a little to the right?'

As she shifted, I understood why this portrait didn't please me. I'd invented her to my expectations, as an artist, as an author. Her literary objectivity had fooled me. I'd heard the hate she'd expressed at my dinner party. Her independent life conflicted with the claims she implied she had on her grown son's heart. The intelligence I admired coexisted with a lonely and possessive passion that insisted I make room for it if my canvas of Ruth was to be real.

★ ★ ★

'We're nearly finished,' I told her a few weeks later as I was packing up. I couldn't stretch out the sessions any longer. The portrait disappointed me but working it over and over was not bringing me closer to a solution. The likeness was reasonable. My commission was fulfilled.

'I hope this doesn't mean the end of you and Heath?' She sounded wistful.

'Why ever would it? You're always welcome here. We enjoy your company.'

'Really?'

'I'd miss you, Ruth. So would Heath. We don't know so many people.'

'Your friends the Scarfs seem like family.'

'That's true. We're older, of course. Heath only opted for music in his thirties. He and Roly did their degrees together. That put the cat among the pigeons!'

'How's that?'

'Heath's parents disapproved. What were we thinking of, throwing away security, two little boys at school? Actually it was the best time of our lives. We were finally getting trained to do what we each loved most, and mixing with students. The Scarfs seemed so unconventional and free. They went off to Europe after Roly qualified — sent back wonderful long letters from French *chateaux* and Italian *pensiones*. I was green with envy.'

'You wanted to travel?'

'Not exactly. But we married so young. I had two kids by the time I was twenty-one.'

'You'd never kicked up your heels?'

'Something like that. When they finally came home and Rowena was trying to drag Roly down the aisle, they'd each run to us with their dilemmas. They do it even now. Our own sons never do.' I fell silent, thinking that neither of my boys knew me as an individual.

'Asher and I are like *that*.' Ruth held up two fingers, interlocked. I wondered how she could be so confident. Of course distance insulates us from reality. I thought back to myself as a narrow and self-centred student. Then, Ruth, in her twenties, would have been in the thick of the Arab-Israeli conflict. Faint resonances of its pain used to issue from radio and newspaper reports but I can't say I was interested. On a map, I'd hardly have known where to point to Egypt, Syria or Palestine. As for Ben Gurion, Nasser, King Hussein, Sadat, Begin . . . They were mysterious names associated with countries far away and over there. Unlike Rowena, I never joined in when Heath and Roly discussed those foreign conflicts. She was young; one couldn't imagine a baby growing inside that flat belly. But one day she'd be a mother like me, with less to say and more to do.

One political crisis after the next slid by. I barely noticed. My interest lay in the colour wheel and my two boys' growth. What had world events to do with me, busy with my hog and sable brushes, my viridian and madder lake? Though I was narrow, self-centred and unaware, I don't berate myself. What a future was there for the taking! We all arm ourselves against life's remorseless lessons; the young with brash confidence, Ruth with memories. She was lucky to have them if they gave her hope and comfort.

One pays dearly for the giving-up of innocence. How we cling to our illusions! Even when they fall, we hang on without knowing. Banished beliefs have their own democracy. Heath often said I was naïve, but was that such a bad thing? What was gained when I finally removed those rose-coloured spectacles he made fun of? I dismissed him from my bed and denied him sex. Well, that was the way I came to judge myself. But Heath had collaborated with me. We came to that moment together. It fell to me to make the announcement and Heath, of course, was devastated, though he'd been driving me away from him for years. He didn't know that and yet, perhaps, he too blamed himself. The religious training he'd rejected wasn't erased. He'd been fed concepts of sin, hell and judgement with his breakfast cereal. Shame lived on; guilt worked away. No wonder the Jesuits gloat that a child trained in their ways at seven belongs to them for life. A terrible knowledge of psychology underlies such power.

Unlike Roly, Heath never flirted. He was that rare man, a faithful husband. I assumed he was virtuous — a better man than most. It never crossed my mind that marriage might be his shark net, holding at bay the lurking monsters of the deep. It never occurred to me that he refused all truck with adult magazines and videos because they might reflect his own desires. He frowned at smut; was modest to the point of locking the bathroom door when he showered. I never wondered why. That was Heath. If anything, I thought I was well off. If he was a little stuffy, at least I wasn't wondering what my husband was up to. I didn't have to watch him make eyes at every pretty woman, as poor Rowena had to do with Roly.

Heath disapproved of his old friend's roaming eye. It pained him to have a son like Joe, who went from one relationship to the next as casually as a fruit picker. I never realised their alignments were complementary, like the hangman's to the condemned. Heath believed he was a free and rational man. He'd buried his childhood, his mother, his church. Of course I had my own illusions. Mistakenly I imagined those lost moments of intimacy wouldn't count. It was a shock to me when I found myself changing from the creative, happy person I believed myself to be. My peace of mind faltered, I became a watcher and suspicion entered in.

7

Straight after breakfast on the morning after that first walk, I donned sun hat and gloves and went out into the garden. Spring showers had softened the earth. Lucky this wasn't the hard-baked soil of December or I would have really had my work cut out. As it was, I could easily clear a couple of square metres by morning tea. It felt good to use my body. Listless days inside the house had done nothing for me. The scratches, aching back and sunburn I could expect from gardening would be a welcome change. The wild growth offered small surprises; dark blue grape hyacinths and droopy narcissus, rather the worse for wear in their struggle towards the light. Winter had killed off a lot of the weed clumps. Their roots yielded easily, and underneath the soil looked rich with moisture and writhing worms. The discard heap began to form a decent mound. It was far too late to prune the roses but they would simply have to survive unseasonable conditions. With secateurs I slashed angled cuts above the strongest-looking leaflets, putting the rose prunings in a separate pile for safe transport to the rubbish bin.

As I worked, I turned over in my mind Ruth's brief message. Now she had made contact, I was uncertain how to react. Did I really want to renew our friendship? If so, she had made the overture. Or was it better to let things lie? Heath was gone. Our threesome no longer existed. It was only in its absence that I realised our whole relationship had been built on the basis of a triangle, not a pair. Even after the portrait sittings ended, it seemed natural to include Ruth in our social life. We made her into a possession we could pass back and forth. Heath might say to me, 'Let's take a run up to the Bay with the girls on Saturday. Does Ruth like picnics?'

'I expect so. Why not give her a call and ask?'

'You talk to her. Here, I'll dial.'

He would hand the phone to me and smile as I reported back. 'She said she'd love to come.'

I remembered one picnic vividly. While Heath selected a wine from his cellar, I packed up cold chicken, egg sandwiches, a Sara Lee cake. Sophie filled the thermos and put cold drinks in the Esky. Vanessa was invited. We would pick her up on our way to Ruth's. Heath and I were cheerful as we loaded the boot. We had a project. The tension was set aside.

We parked outside the Scarfs' run-down house. Rowena, various children in tow, came out to the car. She looked exhausted. Most unusually, Roly was cutting the lawn with an ancient hand mower. It was clear they'd had an argument. He hardly stopped to say hello; attacking the grass with exaggerated, angry pushes as though he was mowing down domestic boredom, restriction and cheeky students all rolled into one. Vanessa piled into the back seat next to Sophie. She was carrying a bag of lemons from their tree.

'I was supposed to make these into some sort of drink but I couldn't be bothered,' she announced cheerfully. 'Mum and Dad had a real blow-up just before you came.'

'I expect your mother needs all the help she can get at present,' I suggested.

'She's a real nag. Poor Dad!'

Clearly she felt a teenager's partisanship with her father. He'd always favoured her. I think her talent made up to him for the disappointments in his own career.

We collected Ruth, who lived in Tighes Hill, not far from the Industrial Highway, and headed out towards the Bay. I was used to the route, but Ruth's keen eye renewed my own pleasure in the countryside. Heath was in a good mood, slowing to allow side-road traffic

136

onto the highway and merely smiling when teenagers passed us like bandits on the run, their old car piled high with surfboards. We decided against the popular beaches. Heath remembered a quiet spot we hadn't visited for years. As we approached I saw how development had moved in. The ramshackle squats and cottages were gone; replaced by imposing waterfront residences whose drawn curtains and locked gates suggested wealthy owners with real lives elsewhere. The place was no doubt crowded during holidays but at present the dunes and beach were almost deserted.

'This do us?' Heath nosed the car into a glade of gums beside the tidal river where two ducks, travelling with purpose, paddled over the brackish surface while a third stood up on the water and fanned its wings. Mosquitoes swarmed in as soon as we climbed out of the car. We sprayed repellent as the girls ran ahead to investigate.

Ruth accepted the can and smiled at me. 'The Aussie aroma! When I went to my first barbecue I thought you all used perfume or aftershave made from some local disinfectant. Heath, do you want a hand?'

He was tramping ahead with rugs and picnic basket, disturbing a grey and pink whirr of galahs. Tall wildflowers were massed in clumps along the riverbank. Ruth snapped a stalk.

'Some variety of ginger?'

'I'd say so. Watch out for ants.'

We settled ourselves on the picnic rug. I lay back assessing the scene from the unusual angle. Adjusting the horizon line could sometimes create interest in quite an ordinary view. I could hear bees humming in the ginger and the trickle of the brackish river.

'This is rather idyllic,' Ruth decided. 'We used to take picnics into the hills near Galilee. What a nature painter's heaven! Acres in bloom; white and yellow and purple and red. Wild rosemary. The scent of rosemary always transports me home.'

'Sounds beautiful. You must get homesick.'

'It wasn't all beautiful.' She was pensive. 'We went hiking one weekend. I was nineteen. My boyfriend was still serving his call-up. I hardly knew him really. My parents disapproved but I was rebellious. Keyed-up. Trouble was brewing. That was 1967.'

Heath nodded. 'The six day David and Goliath war?'

'It hadn't broken. But you could feel it in the air. Life's heightened by crisis.'

'So that's why you remember those wildflowers so vividly?'

'It was my first time with a man. We both

seemed to know it might never happen again.'

'He died?' Heath asked quietly.

'A sniper got him.'

'How do you live with such memories?' I pressed her hand, though she gave no sign she felt my touch.

'That's Israel's reality. I assure you I wasn't alone. Every family seemed to lose someone. We've never stopped fighting off one invader or another.'

She rattled off *Philistines, Assyrians, Greeks, Romans, Arabs, English, French, Ottoman Turks*, as though those ancient oppressions were still real and present in her life. It was all very well for me, I supposed. Australia was the lucky country. I hadn't endured wanton waste of life and loved ones. My time slot saved me. Heath was a child during the Second World War. My boys had escaped the Vietnam ballot. Admittedly, Heath's family was thick with ex-servicemen who took it as fact that they'd met the supreme challenge of being prepared to die for their country. I couldn't reconcile their belief with images of boys slain in thousands; children like mine, victims of haphazard campaigns, dead under the blazing sun or cold mud of foreign battle-fields. To me, the fallen hero was an illusion and a waste. It was a subject Heath and I avoided. My father had been a pacifist. His had gone to war.

'My Dad was at Gallipoli,' said Heath. 'The story goes that he went off at seventeen and came home with white hair.'

Ruth shrugged. 'You're one of the lucky ones if all you lose is the colour of your hair.'

'Of course it went deeper. He was shell-shocked. Never fully recovered. Unpredictable moods. Nightmares. I reckon he could have been a gambler; played cards and darts. But he'd never go near a racetrack. Horses terrified him. He'd heard the screams when they were wounded.'

'You never told me that,' I said.

'War's in the too-hard basket for us to talk about. Life's sweetness and light, isn't that right, Barbie?'

As usual he was joking but I felt hurt to be made fun of like that in front of Ruth. She chose her words carefully. 'No one likes to dwell on humanity's worst behaviour. But innocence can be dangerous too.'

'What do you mean?' I asked her.

'We can't deny that the dark side's never far away.'

Her pensive expression excluded me. No doubt she was thinking of her life before she migrated. I thought war solved nothing but she had actively participated as a soldier.

I knew little of her formative years in Israel.

I'd never had to bear the image of my lover's body bleeding in some dusty alley. What did I know about the Jews' history or the conflicts raised when they returned to Israel? — a few documentaries on SBS or news items that flashed past like a speeding train. Already I'd enjoyed almost three times her young man's life span. Yet I couldn't say I'd made any real contribution to the world. All at once I felt bleak, as though the rest would be only dissolution and the grinding away of fate. I wanted more. But what, when we sat so comfortably, while the river lapped and rippled and the others began to chat together on a lighter note?

I felt like an outsider. It wasn't only their views on war that set them apart. Nothing in my life had ever made me see myself as different. I'd had an ordinary Anglican upbringing and I went to an average state school. Heath, on the other hand, was a Catholic who had deliberately rejected his prospects of salvation. Ruth was a Jew and, while she might be secular, had been passionately involved in Israel's survival from the first moment she drew breath. The two of them were allies. I sat in silence while they argued good-naturedly.

'But consider the Palestinians. How fair was the UN mandate when that land had been their home for centuries?'

'So you have no sympathy with the aboriginal viewpoint? You'd just say, *Stuff them, my great-grandfather had every right to occupy their territory?*

'I never implied it was that simple, Ruth.'

'No, neither did I. I had plenty of reasons for leaving my country.'

'It's a bad moment when you can't resolve conflict except by walking away.'

'It's a moment of despair. You'd know, if you left your church.'

Heath nodded. 'It was painful at the time. That was a long time ago. Burgundy or Rosé?'

'Burgundy please.' Ruth proffered her empty glass with a smile.

I felt excluded and tried to joke it off. 'I'll leave you both to your suffering.'

They both looked at me, and I decided to walk off my irritation. 'I'm going to find the girls, then we'll eat. You two finish the wine.'

I turned from their puzzled faces and walked to the beach, where a salty breeze soon whisked away my crossness. Carrying my sandals, I scuffed along barefoot, kicking up warm grains as I headed into damp sand where my tracks followed the paw imprints of a dog I could see silhouetted far down the beach. The girls must have gone round the headland. I wandered in that direction, competing with little waves as they rose and broke in measured rhythm and sluiced over heaps of kelp. The sun was a hazy disc of brightness. I squinted, noting the forms of two children playing in the water near the rocks. A man sat watching them; keeping an eye on their safety, I assumed, for they were only little girls, not more than five- or six-year-olds. Giggling and shrieking, their play made me recall those long, innocent hours one had spent discovering the magic of shells and stones, or dreamily floating in a safe warm rock pool.

Some intentness about the trio made them unaware of my approach. First one then the other girl sprang upright and splashed down in a kind of abandoned dance. The children were stark naked. I could feel the man's absorption, and sense his mood change when he noticed me. He gestured roughly until they both bobbed back under the water. I turned instinctively and retraced my path, carrying with me a sense of shock and strange guilt. I felt I'd disturbed a scene not meant for my eyes.

Sophie and Vanessa were slithering down the dunes as I began to walk back to the glade.

'Where were you, Nan?'

'Stretching my legs before lunch. Aren't you hungry?'

They were. Already Ruth and Heath had started laying out the picnic plates. I began to unpack the food, waving away the flies that are part and parcel of every Australian picnic. I told myself this was a happy family outing. But as we all sat down to eat I felt confused. Small children played naked on every sundrenched beach. Why did my mind's eye refuse to forget the image of two lithe young bodies and a man's predatory stillness as he gazed at them? For me, the day was spoiled. I wasn't sorry when Heath suggested it was time we make tracks for home.

We dropped Ruth and Vanessa off at their respective doors. There was a message on the answerphone from Roly when we arrived home. He'd had to take Rowena in to hospital. She'd been admitted for assessment and bed rest. Criticism of her mother forgotten, Vanessa phoned us. She was obviously upset by the scribbled note her father had left.

'Let's get the facts,' I suggested, and I dialled to make enquiries. Rowena wasn't in labour by the sound of things. Roly phoned us within the hour. He was back at home.

'They want her in until the baby comes. Blood pressure's too high. She has to rest.'

I couldn't see that eventuating if she went home and said so.

'I should have done more to help.'

Poor penitent Roly, who'd never made a bed or done a load of washing in his life!

I spoke to Heath. 'How will he manage all those children?'

Heath shrugged as though domestic matters saw to themselves the way grass grew and bulbs popped through the earth. However, he came up with a workable idea.

'Why not send Sophie over to stay? She and Vanessa are capable girls.'

I agreed. The girls would enjoy being together. I began to plan a batch of quick-freeze cooking. My energy surged and the unpleasant memories of the beach faded. Someone needed me. Of course Sophie was entranced by our proposal.

'I'll be able to cook, and do the washing and ironing.'

I had to smile. Once the idea of setting up house had thrilled me too. Life had knocked the excitement out of Shepherd's Pie and creased shirts. But I could remember the urge to nest.

'What's easy to cook, Nan?'

'Now wait a minute. I have to check this out with Roly.'

'Oh, he must say yes! He'll be grateful.'

'You go and make your room tidy while I enquire.'

Though I was pretty sure Roly would jump at the offer. And responsibility would do Sophie good. Raised like an only child in our affluent home, she had no idea how well off she was.

She was sitting back on her heels, flushed with accomplishment, when I went to give her the good news. A hurricane appeared to have swept through every drawer and cupboard in her room. I found a small space on the bed and idly scanned her *Save* pile; music awards, exam results, school reports, her First Aid certificate, the debating trophy, concert programmes, photos. A bundle of postcards, tied with a ribbon, were from her mother.

'May I see?'

She nodded. I scanned the faded photos of jacaranda trees in Grafton and rainbow lorikeets at Mount Warning National Park. The scrawled messages were brief. *Hi honey! How's it going? Hope to see you real soon. Miss you heaps.* Expressionless, I gave them back to her and she carefully retied the ribbon. Invisible between those lines was Joe's hurt, my grandchild's bewilderment, and our own disrupted life.

Sophie was watching me. 'I wonder where

she is? Do you know?'

I shook my head. 'No I don't.'

'When I was little, I used to think she'd died. If there were floods I'd think she'd drowned. Or burned to death when they had bush fires on the news. If I heard about a car crash or a murder, I'd think it was her.'

'I don't doubt she's alive and well.'

'Dad told me a bit about her when he was here. He said they met in Tahiti.'

'Well, you knew that.'

'Yes. So I used to tell the kids at school my mother was a Tahitian princess and she'd had to go back home to be a queen.'

I laughed.

'Well, she'd gone somewhere. And she had long dark hair, and brown skin. I think.'

'She was a beach chick — I think that was the expression for a person who put a lot of effort into their tan.' More than she ever gave to her husband or child, I thought.

'I pretended I would steal the money and run away to Tahiti to find her.'

Gently I tried to tell Sophie what her mother had been. 'She was just a young, immature Australian girl, not much older than you when she met Joe. She was on holiday when he was touring with the band.'

'Why doesn't she write to me, Nan?'

She spoke so wistfully I felt guilty. Those

rare postcards used to so unsettle the little girl that finally I'd sent one back, address unknown, and there'd been no more. I stood up briskly.

'Better to forget her, Sophie. If you're going to Vanessa's, pack up this mess.' I viewed the heap of stretched knickers, holey sneakers, mouldy lunch packets, dog-eared study notes, singlets she refused to wear and clothes I'd last seen when she was twelve. 'Put any wearable clothes in a charity bag. Mrs. L. can use the rest as dusters.'

Heath offered to drive us over to the Scarfs' after tea.

'Got your music, young lady? Remember, the exam's not far off.'

'I promise I'll practise.'

'What's in this bag — a body?'

Sophie just laughed exuberantly. You'd have thought she was setting off for Europe.

When we arrived, Vanessa was putting the younger children to bed while Roly watched the news. Sophie didn't want us to hang about. I waved as Heath started up the car, but she had already gone inside.

★ ★ ★

A week or so later, as Mrs. L. and I were cleaning windows, I had a call from Rowena.

She had signed herself out of hospital. She wasn't in the mood to listen to my advice.

'I'll rest. I'll be all right.' She was a tiger defending her cubs. 'This baby isn't ready to be born.'

'How long to go?'

The date she mentioned was the same as Sophie's sixteenth birthday. Perhaps there would be cause for a double celebration.

'You know you can call on me, day or night.'

'Thanks, Barb.' She did sound relaxed. Perhaps lying in hospital worrying about her children could well be more stressful than actually being home with them. Surely Roly would pitch in, and Vanessa would help.

'My friend's out of hospital.' I knew Mrs. L. had been listening avidly to the conversation. 'I suppose Sophie will be coming home tonight.'

'I'll vacuum her room, once we finish these windders.'

She stood back, hands on hips, sweat beading her lined, honest face. 'There! That's better. Nothing like nice clean glass to put a bit of sparkle in a place.'

After my help had departed I went to check on Sophie's room. It had an unused stuffiness and I pushed up the window. A stiff breeze caught the curtains, sending papers flying off the desk. I hadn't noticed them before; Mrs. L. must have uncovered them in some dusty corner. Casually I glanced at the pages. Sophie was a vivid storyteller, though her poems and stories were often overblown. She would learn to edit in time; better she felt deeply, I thought. Of course she could be as sulky as any teenager at times, but her writing struck me as the expression of a deep and generous heart.

But as I read my face grew hot and my heart began to race. Dazed, I read the page again. It was torn from an exercise book and was evidently part of some longer project; perhaps an attempt to write a sexy romance? I was shocked by the lurid details of her erotic language. She hadn't learned this sort of thing in biology class. I wanted to crumple the page and toss it in the incinerator but this was Sophie's handwriting; this was my granddaughter's mind. Why would she write about an older man? A man with fatherly attributes, a man in a position of authority? The girl in question was not a victim, except that she was less than half her seducer's age. But how willing she was to be initiated and how eagerly she responded to every sexual fantasy her childish handwriting could cram onto a page of foolscap. The last sentence was incomplete, as though her inventive mind had finally run out of ideas.

I bundled the papers and shoved them under a pile of old school-books. I locked the window and went to get myself a glass of water. I was relieved that Heath was out on some errand. I was sure my shock was visible. Where could Sophie have learned about such sexual practices? Who was the seducer in her story? I thought of our single beds. Was this Heath's answer to celibacy?

I paced the house, my imagination running wild. I pictured the two of them in the kitchen, standing close as they washed the dishes. I saw them alone in the music room, Sophie's fingers on the keys, Heath's hand closing over hers. Sinister now, that silence between notes; that stillness behind closed doors. I went into the bedroom and sat down on my bed, remembering Heath's look of disbelief and sorrow when I told him our sexual life was over. Was Sophie the substitute he'd turned to, or could I have been ignorant for years? One heard these awful things discussed on TV programmes. There were stories in magazines. Could I possibly be married to a lecher who lusted for a child? I ran from the house to the only retreat I had, shut the door of my studio and wept. At first the tears were an outpouring without thought or reason. They came from a sadness so deep

I could not give it words. It seemed I had let it build for a lifetime. A record existed of every single hurt, disappointment, rejection, failure, emptiness and this was the score — Barbie, weeping. I knew the page of writing was no more than a catalyst. Sophie had probably heard there was a fortune to be made in writing porn but her words were after all no worse than the graffiti scratched on lavatory doors. Any enterprising teenager could get hold of seedy magazines and videos so openly displayed in shops, and even literature seemed to delight in drug and sex scenarios. She wasn't our prisoner and she had to cope in her own world and make her own mistakes. Sex was hardly the deep secret it used to be. Perhaps I'd used it to play psychological games with my husband and now my own guilt had backfired on me. I had assumed far too much about Heath.

His image stood before me, defenceless and accused. There had never been the slightest sign that he had improper designs on any student. How could I have placed him in the role of Sophie's seducer? I hated myself for thinking such thoughts about him. When I heard his car, my heart began to thump and I wanted to hide from him. But he was coming in the back entrance. The garage door rattled. I heard the car door slam. He was walking along the garden path towards the studio. The white rose was in flower and he stopped and plucked a bloom, avoiding thorns. I heard his cheerful greeting. 'Are you working, Barbie?'

★ ★ ★

Reluctantly I opened the door, hoping my face did not look too ravaged. He smiled and held out the flower.

'Well, that all went well. I mentioned Consumer Affairs, and the sales people became very pally. Agreed to replace the thermostat free of charge. So I should think.' He paused. 'You look upset.'

'A headache coming on.'

'Come inside and take a break. I'll put the kettle on. What about a sandwich?'

'That might be nice.' I walked beside him, noticing his step was slower and heavier than it used to be.

'Are you tired?'

'I don't know why I should be. Let's both have a lie down before the students descend.'

'Yes. Sophie will be home later.' I told him about Rowena.

'Typical woman. Thinks the world will fall apart without her.'

'I think she should have stayed in hospital too.' For once I felt submissive.

While he taught that afternoon, I tried to rest. Roly dropped Sophie off later.

'I'm so glad to be home! What's for dinner?'

I had to laugh. Keeping house had apparently worn thin. She looked tired.

'Late nights?'

'It's pretty rowdy at the Scarfs.'

'What about a bath and an early night?'

She seemed to enjoy being fussed over like a little girl. 'I missed you, Nan.'

She hugged me warmly and I knew she still needed me to help and guide her, encourage her dreams and protect her in any way I could.

I'd faced my suspicions and I thought that would be the end of it. We were the same happy little family group we'd always been. Yet in the weeks that followed, I found the dark thoughts coming back to ambush me when I was least expecting them. During a music lesson I would walk in to the studio without my usual courtesy knock. There they'd be, Sophie and Heath, studiously working through a theory paper.

'Just wondered if you'd like a cup of tea.'

Heath would smile with pleasure. 'Thoughtful of you. All this talk makes me dry.'

One day I even heard myself quiz Sophie. 'Done any writing lately?'

'Only my history assignment. Do you know about the Peloponnesian wars, Nan?'

'No, Sophie. I expect every war is much the same . . . Lies, betrayals, secrets.'

I saw her puzzled face before I turned and walked away.

★　★　★

Everyday life went on. Mrs. L. came on Monday. On Friday, we did the banking and went out to lunch. A new Chinese place had opened on the waterfront and trade at *Lims'* had fallen off. As we walked through the plastic fly strips in the doorway, a fragile girl who ought to have been at school almost ran to pull out chairs and hand us menus. Our order never varied. Heath would have Lemon Chicken and I Braised Vegetables with Cashews. We'd share steamed rice and ask for cutlery instead of chopsticks. Heath would order a light beer and I a glass of cask Moselle.

The girl scurried away with our order as I surveyed the other deserted tables.

'I hope they don't go broke. They work so hard and for so little return.'

'People say the new place is better.'

'They were quite happy to eat here before. There's no loyalty these days.'

155

Heath just shrugged. 'The market dictates who survives.'

His indifference infuriated me. 'That's what I said, Heath!'

I had raised my voice. The waitress coming with our drinks paused, not wanting to intrude on an argument. I smiled at her warmly. 'Very prompt service here. We love the food.'

'Thank you. Meals coming now.'

'They get the prize for quick cuisine; hope it's not leftovers.'

'You know perfectly well there are health regulations.'

He just raised his glass in a genial gesture. Lately my moods seemed to pass him by. When the food arrived we shared it out and began to eat. I was glad to have my mouth full. It took away the need for conversation. How had we ever chatted so easily? I sat in silence, full of fears I couldn't talk about and questions I couldn't ask. Through the plate glass window, toddlers dragged on reins, shoppers hurried past, an off-lead puppy scooted in and out of passers-by. Once we used to make up stories about the regulars, like the Salvation Army collector and the anorexic man who walked like a fakir in a trance. Now I ate in silence.

'Chicken's a bit stringy,' Heath suggested.

'Nothing wrong with mine.'

He tried again. 'How's the portrait?'

'I've told Ruth that I don't need any more sittings.' At least I could talk about work. 'I'm disappointed though . . . I feel like painting over it and starting again from scratch.'

'Why? I thought it was a good likeness.'

'Yes. It's just not Ruth.'

'Ah! I could tell you had some worry on your mind.'

So that's what he thought. I was moody because of an unsatisfactory piece of work. How did such gulfs grow? My husband was checking the bill as he always did. Why did I feel I sat opposite a stranger; or worse, an enemy?

8

I had few visitors in the months that followed Heath's death. It was as though I had become invisible, even to myself. I couldn't imagine entering a room alone when we had always been a couple, and I had turned down several invitations. After a while people left me alone. Alex was my only regular caller. Perhaps he'd put me on his duty list. *Book clients, prepare quarterly tax return, check on Mother.* But he did call in once a week and even cut the grass for me.

'You're making an impression on the garden, aren't you?' He stood surveying the front yard and I realised how much I missed that companionable sense of working as a team.

'I've put in seedlings. Phlox there, and cosmos, the tall ones. I'd like to replace that camellia with something smaller. Perhaps I'll get you to dig it out one day.'

'Is there really any point?'

My son was reminding me I would have to sell my home. I couldn't imagine him listening quietly to my confused thoughts. Like Heath, he would offer plans and

158

solutions I wasn't ready to hear.

'Perhaps not. Have you time for a quick coffee before you go?'

'I'm in no hurry,' he said, surprising me. 'Helen's away for a few days.'

Something was amiss. 'In Sydney, shopping?'

'With her parents. Some sort of 'flu, apparently.'

'I've heard there's a spring epidemic.'

I knew him well enough to see he felt abandoned. Helen had never moved out of home before. 'Well, let me know when the crisis has passed.'

'I will.'

'And you're managing?'

'Fine, thanks.' It was his turn to withdraw.

Oh well. Those were the games we played. Helen's visits were just as stilted. She never stayed for coffee; just dropped off cheese scones or a little casserole neatly sealed in plastic wrap. I wondered why I found it so hard to relate to her when she tried to show me kindness. When I was a young wife, I'd have welcomed an understanding mother-in-law. I could make more effort. When she did come home, I would make a point of inviting her to lunch.

'Are you painting again, Mother?' Alex asked as I fixed sandwiches to go with the coffee.

'I haven't touched a brush for six months.' In fact, I'd finished nothing since Ruth's portrait. 'The garden's my priority, and my daily walk.'

My stamina had increased and I went further every week. We'd lived in this outlying suburb for so long I took for granted the peaceful outlook of water, hills and bush. Since last year's tragedy I avoided the lake path. Instead I always went uphill towards the quarry, noting the changes week by week. *Deposit Taken* notices replaced previous *For Sale* signs. Trim gardens reverted to weeds and shorn lawns grew thick as legal processes went on. The skeleton of Banksia Grove Estate loomed large.

When I wasn't walking or gardening, I knew I should be making plans. My nest egg was dwindling. The estate agent had phoned back, inquiring when I would be ready to sell. Alex issued hints each time he came. But there was something I had to clarify and I clasped my home around me like a mantle while I racked my brains, going over and over events. A year ago I'd had a husband, I'd had close friends. Now everyone had gone. At times my thoughts were self-pitying and I wept. Then I cast myself as instigator of it all, and the others were just accomplices. For I thought each of us tended to believe our worst actions were excusable and necessary. Evil doers and fanatics no doubt had logical explanations for their crimes. Of course I loved Heath, yet at times I hated him. Would he be alive today if I hadn't tried to force out of him words he couldn't speak, and feelings he didn't want to share?

Well, he'd really left me now. It wasn't only Heath I'd lost. The Scarfs were gone. How I missed Rowena! We'd been such friends. I remembered visiting her not long before the last baby's birth. She was still on strict bed rest. She took my magazines with a listless hand.

'Roly and the kids are making an effort, but I loathe this lying around.' Her complexion had that brown cast you see on some pregnant women.

'Was Sophie a help while you were away?' I'd been curious about my granddaughter's housekeeping efforts.

'No serious mishaps — some of the sheets have a mysterious pink tinge and there were strange concoctions in the fridge.'

We both laughed. 'We all learn the hard way. She's been strange since she came home. Withdrawn.' Privately I wondered if Sophie was missing young company. Heath and I must seem old-fashioned to a teenager.

'She's only fifteen, Barb. Weren't you

moody at that age?'

'Of course. I found something she'd written, very sexual, actually I was shocked.'

'I loved reading bodice-rippers at her age.' Rowena was laughing. 'Didn't you?'

'I don't think so. I haven't said anything to her yet.'

'Don't. You'll embarrass her. She won't thank you for spying.'

'I wasn't! I found it quite by accident.'

'She won't believe that. Anyway, what's the harm in writing about sex? If she's actually doing it your worries will begin! I'm wondering whether Vanessa should go on the Pill.'

'Rowena!'

'Barbie, you're the proverbial ostrich. Vanessa and Sophie are young women.'

'They're under age.'

'Twelve-year-olds have babies. We live in the modern world.'

Why did people keep saying that to me? They seemed to be advising me to accept sex and drugs as natural progressions for adolescents. But I didn't want to get into an argument when Rowena was supposed to be resting. Suddenly she reached for my hand and pressed it to her abdomen.

'Lively little brat! Can't wait to get her out of me.'

'I've never seen a baby born.'

162

'Then come to the delivery.'

'Would I be allowed?'

'I'll say we're sisters. God, I can't wait to get it over. This is definitely Rowena Scarf's last stand.'

'You've said that before.'

'No, I mean it this time. Come if you want. I'd like you to be there, Barb.'

How happy her casual invitation made me! Of course the prospect of welcoming the littlest Scarf into the world pleased me. But it was Rowena's willingness to share her intimate pain and joy that proved we were true friends.

★   ★   ★

My life seemed so rich in friendship at that time. The same week, Ruth phoned.

'It's high time you and Heath came to lunch,' she said.

'We'd love to. We'll bring those boxes of music.' She'd taken up his offer of a little work, sorting and mending his treasure-trove of sheet music. I was curious to meet her in her own surroundings. One of the failings of my portrait, I'd decided, was that mentally I'd placed Ruth in my own middleclass, suburban setting. Her real life involved Israel, war, migration, and now a struggle to make ends meet. No wonder the woman on my canvas seemed undefined.

She lived in an inner-city suburb of treeless back streets and light industries. At a railway crossing we waited five minutes while an interminable line of coal hoppers trundled past. Faded, narrow houses leaned close, seeming to prop one another up; one good shove would surely topple their crooked paling fences. Rusty vehicles lined the gutters and I could tell Heath was apprehensive about parking out on the street.

'After lunch I'll take a run into town and leave you two to chin wag,' he suggested.

Ruth's doorbell didn't work. Our knock set off hysterical barking and we stepped backwards as she opened the door and a skinny red setter came flying at us.

'You never said you had a dog.'

'She's a fugitive. We adopted each other in the park last week.'

'Why not send her to the RSPCA?' Heath wasn't a dog man. In his family, animals involved disease and disinfectant and were firmly banished to the outdoors.

'My darling's been half starved. You can see that. But I'll soon fatten her up.'

With adoring eyes the dog tracked her inside, while Heath began to carry in the music piles.

I followed Ruth. Threadbare matting lined the narrow passage. Brown stains blotched the old-fashioned wallpaper. A musty smell whisked me back half a century to unwilling family visits with remote aunts and uncles whose days began and ended in similar gloom. In the living room, listless banners curtained the windows. The fireplace, which might have cheered a drab room, was boarded up with masonite. The furniture was a motley assortment. A battered piano stood in the corner, its amber-yellow ivories defaced with childish ABCs. I walked over and pressed down a few keys.

Ruth touched the crazed polish ruefully. 'This poor old girl was destined for the tip. The tuning pins have had it and the strings are rusty as hell. I offered the people $20 and they were so pleased someone wanted her they even delivered free.'

Heath staggered in with the music cartons. Ruth told him to stack them in the corner. 'These will keep me busy.'

'A few more to come.'

'Wherever does he get it all?' she asked when he had gone.

'Garage sales. Second-hand shops. School fairs. He can't resist a bargain.'

She laughed and began to glance through one of the boxes. I stood, compelled and

165

fascinated by the memories called up by this room. Sent off to the piano while my elders sipped and gossiped, I would reluctantly perform. Stumbling minuets and halting gavottes became inextricably tied in with unlived lives. How glad I used to feel when, duty done, I was dismissed out of earshot, my reward a stale chocolate biscuit.

'Do you play at all?' Ruth was asking.

'Only as a child. I was no musician. Couldn't wait to give it up.'

'It's funny, isn't it? One child's delight can be another's nightmare. I studied for ten years. Loved it. We had a wonderful Boesendorfer. Privileged, I guess — taken to concerts from an early age. Oh, there'd be great excitement, queuing to hear the famous names. Of course I'd wriggle and doze off but the artistry got through. My father was well known so we'd be allowed backstage to have our programme autographed. I'd earn a smile and a pat on the head.'

'You must have left a lot behind in Israel?'

'I travelled light. For heaven's sake, what am I thinking of? Sit down, make yourself comfortable. It's no palace but it's home. Are you hungry? I made some traditional food for you both to try.'

She was a different person in her own environment. I suppose we all adjust our persona to suit our company. Here, she was domesticated, garrulous, a devoted animal lover. She was fondling the setter's ears gently, in the way she'd touched the piano. Squatting on bony haunches, the dog surveyed her with grave brown eyes.

'The food smells delicious.'

'I'll get ready to serve, shall I? Here comes Heath with the last load.'

A small table was set with odd bits of china and glasses. An unusual candelabrum formed the centrepiece. I asked her about it.

'It's a menorah. I keep it for sentiment. It's used in religious ceremonies as a rule. But I'm just a *sabra* . . . Israeli-born Jew.'

'I would never have picked it.'

'I don't fit with *Fiddler on the Roof*? When I arrived in this country I had a touch of the cork-brimmed hat and kangaroo syndrome myself.'

The colourful cloth and serviettes had an ethnic look. 'Did you bring these with you?'

'I embroidered them. One of my hobbies.'

Appetising dishes were arriving from the kitchen. 'Hope you like these. Humus — that's pureed chickpeas. Tahini. And felafels.'

The dog, assuming it was also invited to the meal, sat next to Heath, panting eagerly and salivating on his shoe. He edged it aside, none too gently, as Ruth brought in the last plates.

'She hasn't learned table manners. Here, Beth!' She tossed a small fried meatball in the air. Beth gulped it down and slithered on her belly to Ruth's feet, where she settled, gently gnawing on a chair leg. Heath cleared his throat and began to help himself to the various cuisines.

'Who's for wine?'

'I have a few calls to make in town.' But Heath edged his glass forward and Ruth smiled at him. 'One won't put you over the limit.'

She'd gone to a lot of trouble with the meal. The flavours were spicy and delicious. We became involved in a lively discussion on ethnic cooking. I reminded Heath of our own provincial upbringing and he nodded.

'Dining out was roast lamb and apple pie at the pub.'

'Starched white cloths and a jug of water on the table.'

'Waitresses in black frocks and white aprons. Heath, remember we used to go to Fry's for Polish salami and fetta cheese? We thought we were frightfully modern.'

'Tradition shapes us all,' Ruth agreed. 'None more so than my own dear race.'

After lunch Heath pushed back his chair.

'Come on, Ruth; I'll give you a quick run-down on how I'd like the music filed.'

I sat sipping my wine, reflecting on our student days. We'd been a privileged group, unaware and smug, although such a suggestion would have upset us greatly. No aboriginals or migrants attended the conservatorium or Art School. Greeks and Italians moved among us, enlivening the streets with their dress and language, but we didn't mix. We were the stars. They were the extras who poured the concrete, painted the houses and laboured in the filthy industries that hovered beyond our awareness while we embraced poverty, or our idea of it, heating baked beans on the gas ring and singing along with Joan Baez to *We Shall Overcome*. But what had we ever had to fight for? We'd never known hardship. Naturally everyone wanted to go overseas. What was in dull old Newcastle? Faces glistening with sweat and coal dust. Nothing worth painting. Who'd be able to develop vision here!

The dog began a determined inspection of Heath's crotch. Abruptly he stood up. 'I'll get going. Be about an hour. You two have fun.'

'I'll see you out.'

'No, no. Just hold on to the animal.' He waved and went. Ruth was smiling after him.

'He's an attractive man. You're a lucky woman, Barb.'

I considered her words as I drained my wine. *Attractive?* I felt flattered, as though she'd credited me with good taste.

'I guess Heath's aged well.'

'Aged? I don't see him in that light.'

'How do you see him?'

'Oh, I liked him straight away.'

There was an atmosphere in the room. I felt she was trying to broach something with me.

'There's no man in your own life now?'

She shrugged. 'My divorce was bitter, on both sides. You think twice about jumping back into the fire.'

So she had been married. She reached out and began to stroke the emaciated dog as though the pair had loneliness in common. How readily she had accepted our invitations to share our social life.

'Don't get me wrong,' she went on. 'I admire Heath. I quite fancy him, to tell the truth. But it's obvious he's not that type. He thinks the world of you.'

'Why are you telling me this?' Though it seemed somehow right that Ruth, with her isolated life, her ancient piano and only a stray dog to share her affection, would confide in me.

'Secretive longings are for the young, don't you think?' She laughed. 'More wine?'

Idly I offered my glass. 'I don't remember having secretive attachments.'

'Come on! You've never strayed?'

'I'm not aware that I have . . . '

'It's when we're innocent and unaware that the trouble starts.'

I didn't want her to speak to me in that knowing way, as though I was a fool.

'Getting back to these secretive attachments; are you attached to Heath?'

'Sometimes I do think about him.'

This extraordinary turn in the talk, coupled with too much wine, was confusing.

Ruth smiled at me appealingly. She'd taken a risk in talking to me like that. I decided I didn't mind. Intimacy wasn't tender emotion born of candlelight and soft words. It came roughly, tearing down a façade. You might try to put that protective barrier back in place but, once fallen, there it stayed.

'You're not upset, are you?' she asked.

'I was just thinking. No, I'm not upset. A bit surprised.' She raised her dark eyebrows. 'I just don't think of Heath like that.' On reflection, how did I think of him? I took him for granted, when he wasn't annoying me.

'If you don't, someone else will.' She spoke lightly, but I wondered whether she was

171

trying to advise me. Could she possibly know about our situation? Perhaps she'd wondered about the single beds in our room, or picked up on the abrasive note between us. She was a writer, sensitive to nuance. Or could Heath possibly have dropped a hint of how it was between us?

'We don't sleep together,' I heard myself saying. 'Not any more.'

'It's none of my business,' Ruth said. But it was my turn to speak honestly.

'We've been married nearly forty years. Life becomes a habit. Most couples seem to accept that. I couldn't. I still want love, affection, tenderness. Do you think that's too much to ask?'

'Of course I don't. I can see Heath's from the old school. Reserved. But he seems very fond of you, Barb. Do you mean there's some sort of health problem?'

'No. Heath likes to blame menopause but that's got nothing to do with it. I'm simply tired of being taken for granted. I want to be needed.'

'So this was your decision?' She sounded doubtful. 'How could withdrawing like that make things better? Wouldn't it have the opposite effect?'

'So I've discovered.'

Was it disloyal of me, passing Heath's

presence back and forth between us like a parcel? We were at opposite ends of the spectrum. Ruth was single. She was free and open to options. She had every right to fantasies of love and desire. Whereas time had eroded all surprise between Heath and myself. How was he to interpret my sexual withdrawal, except as a rejection, when I'd meant it as a passionate demand for change between us?

'Barb? Have I alienated you? I shouldn't have told you how I feel.'

I smiled at her. 'You were honest. I like that. Far too much is left unsaid as a rule. Anyway, I like you. We like you. We're friends, aren't we?'

'Of course. Most people lead such closed, possessive little lives.'

'Let's have coffee. Heath will probably be a while. He had several stops to make.'

She nodded and left me to wonder why I'd been so open, when I hadn't even talked things over with Rowena. But Ruth was penetrating in a way Rowena wouldn't comprehend. And having spoken my thoughts aloud, I knew I would have to be similarly honest with Heath. He mightn't understand but I owed him that much.

By mutual consent, we dropped personal exchanges. With the strong coffee she served *halva*, a sticky confection she'd made herself. While the dog gulped several pieces, Ruth opened her workbag and went on stitching a bright cushion cover, sharing her worries about Asher since the recent flare-ups reported on the news. I tried to imagine how I would feel if Alex and Joe were in the daily firing line of ethnic tensions.

'How do you cope?' I asked her, and wasn't cruel enough to share my own experience of mothers and grown sons when she answered, 'I imagine what we'll do when he comes to Australia to live with me.'

★ ★ ★

Heath soon returned. Ruth suggested afternoon tea, but when the dog leaped up and tried to lick his face, he shook his head.

'No thanks. We'll get going.'

'Not before you play something.'

Heath was nothing if not polite. Ignoring the piano's shortcomings he performed one of Satie's little *Gymnopedies*. The honkytonk effect had the wistful overtones of music drifting from some late-night lonely café.

'Thank you.' She looked happy. 'Promise me you'll come again soon.'

She walked us to the front door, the grip of her fingers on my arm suggesting some

174

unspoken bond. On the way home I sat quietly, thinking back to how I'd also been attracted by Heath's playing; by the way he could turn that worn old piano at the local dance hall into an instrument of energy and romance. Yes, we'd been happy then. Our lovemaking had made us feel close and warm. I was to blame as much as Heath if we had exchanged that for habit, duty, relief, a bargain struck, a boost to ego, a vain demand that one was not yet old and unattractive. We should have both looked deeper and found more to say. Ruth, by revealing herself, had made me face the emptiness within my marriage. Perhaps in some way she had suggested a bridge for me to cross that gulf.

9

Heath and I had a really dreadful row that evening. His pupils came and went until dinnertime. I muddled about in the kitchen, trying to put a meal together. It was as though something extraordinary as an earthquake had shaken me. I was upset and, yes, exhilarated. A safe life is bland. We need our shocks, as the media well knows.

I kept seeing Ruth's serious yet open gaze as she revealed her private feelings. That was very different from the way Heath and I related. Habit, memories, routine bound us. As the clock chimed six, the piano's tinkling would cease. Heath would write out the receipt, hand over change, walk the pupil to the door. He would come into the kitchen, peer at the salad bowl, lift the saucepan lid. Then he would speak.

Which is exactly how it was.

'What's for tea?' He noticed my expression. 'Have I said something funny?'

'Do you know you've said that every night for near on forty years?'

And we were off.

'It's a reasonable question, at dinnertime.'

'Very reasonable.' Bitterly I thrust his plate at him. He sat down, unfolding his serviette in the habitual way and tucking it into his shirtfront. He began on his vegetables, spearing them exactly with his fork, chewing thoroughly, as I was sure his mother had trained him to do.

For a while we ate in silence. The inexpressive set of Heath's face infuriated me. How could I talk about anything that mattered to me? I thought he looked bored and self-absorbed. He set his knife and fork side by side, the fork concave, as it should be when the eater has done with the food.

'Any sweets, Barbie?'

'Rice in the fridge.'

'I threw that out yesterday. It was past the use-by date.'

'Like us.'

'Have you got a headache? Too much wine at Ruth's?'

His complacent smile enraged me. 'No! A heartache.'

Overlooking this *non sequitur*, he took an orange from the fruit bowl and fetched a fresh knife and clean plate. 'Do you want a piece of fruit?' he asked.

I considered myself to be non-violent. For some reason, the sight of that neat little man waiting for my answer, an orange in his hand, sent me over the edge of control. I began to shout at him.

'Our marriage is dead! We never talk! I won't live like this!'

He stood there, reasoning out my words. Apparently they made no sense to him.

'Barbie, why don't we just get dinner over?'

I picked up my plate then and heaved it at the wall. It smashed. China fragments scattered all over the floor. I watched remotely as bright bits of tomato and pumpkin dropped off the wall. It was a strangely satisfying thing to do.

'How dare you ignore me, Heath — why do you do it?'

He looked from me to the mess on the floor. 'Barbie. Just calm down.'

'Don't you patronise me!' He stood, bewildered. 'Put that bloody orange down.'

Slowly he sat down and faced me. 'What's happened? Why are you so upset?'

'You know!' I sounded grim and blaming. 'Just tell me the last time we shared anything remotely real or true or personal?'

At that, a different expression replaced his look of confusion. His tone was cold and triumphant, though his words were measured.

'I think I can do that. It was five and a half months ago.' It was clearly a calculation he checked regularly. 'You might remember. It was you who decided our sex life was over. For good.'

He always covered anger with point-scoring sarcasm. He could switch off emotion like a hardened doctor and I hated him. I watched him rip off his spectacles as though he wanted out-of-focus vision. He sat down, rigid, as though afraid of his own violence. His hand was clenched against me on the table. Objectively my eye recorded the ridged nails, skinny tendons, and several liver spots I'd never noticed. I realised that rejecting fist belonged to a man who was growing old.

'So why would you care so much? We'd almost given up on sex. I can't remember the last time you actually made love to me.'

The silence in the room now felt long and awkward. When he spoke, the words seemed difficult.

'There are a lot of reasons why I care. You're my wife. I married you. I love you. My body still wants you. But I can cope with all that. What I really mind is that this wasn't something *we* decided. We didn't even discuss it, did we? I had no say. This physical condition is yours, not mine. I don't feel what you feel. You don't seem to care one way or another. My lovemaking can't have meant much. Probably I bored you. I've become boring. You say so yourself — my routine, my roster, dinner on the table at six o'clock, the way my ailments get on your nerves. I can't help it. What have I done wrong? I can't deal with all this. I don't know what to do.'

He covered his eyes and sat there, hunched, defeated.

I couldn't remember him ever sharing his inadequacies like that. Let Heath discuss concepts, ideas, values, morals, and he'd talk the leg off an iron pot. Otherwise you had to read him.

His words moved me deeply. 'I'm still your wife. But something's been wrong for a long time. Something very slow, insidious. It's been like a thermometer, our marriage. The temperature's crept down and down until you're so cold, chilled to the bone, you have to do something or you'll die. You've seen it with your parents. I saw it with mine. We've only been like them. You haven't done anything wrong.'

He put on his glasses and looked at me. 'Then how can I make it right? What do you want?'

'I need . . . ' I could only register confusion. My life, defined by its roles of wife, mother, daughter, artist, was rushing headlong towards a future of dependent old age and death. It wasn't enough.

'You need . . . ?'

'I don't know!'

If only I could have given him an order form, a shopping list. I'm sure he would have done anything to restore our life to the way it used to be.

He had to go and give a lesson after dinner. I packed up the dishes, gathered the broken china and sponged the food marks off the wall. Sophie came home as I was washing up. She'd been to the Scarfs' and I asked how Rowena was.

'OK I think.' She hardly seemed to register the question.

'Would you like to invite Vanessa for the weekend?' To my surprise she shrugged indifferently.

'Have you two had a disagreement?'

'Nope.'

She went to her room and shut the door. That was that.

Heath sat up late, working away on his computer. Although I went to bed, I couldn't sleep. I wasn't sorry we'd had that fight but nothing had been resolved. Perhaps I wanted the impossible. Heath was merely being himself.

★ ★ ★

There must have been mischief in the aspects of the planets that night. I'd dozed off when Heath stood beside me, shaking me awake.

'Roly just phoned.' He touched the bedside lamp and a soft glow suffused the room. 'They've rushed Rowena in to hospital.'

'The baby's coming?'

'Some problem. They're doing a Caesarean.'

'I've never heard of that, with a seventh baby.'

'He sounded very worried.'

'Well, Roly never copes in emergencies.' I meant to lighten our exchange but my heart was beating anxiously for my best friend and the unpredictable risks that hover over every birth.

'He said he'd phone back as soon as it's over.'

'Rowena asked me to attend the birth, you know.'

'Isn't that a strange request?'

'Not really. Not among women in most societies. I was looking forward to it.'

'We won't get much sleep until we get that call. It shouldn't be long — they were wheeling her to theatre when he rang. How about I put the kettle on?'

I felt a rush of gratitude for his practical make-up. Sometimes others' troubles put one's own life in perspective. I lay thinking back to my own boys' births. I'd read a book or two and thought I knew it all. But Joe hadn't been a good experience. I'd lost a few pints of blood. Mainly, I was bewildered. The books had lied. They'd promised me a profound and wonderful experience. But childbirth wasn't natural at all. I'd nearly died, and so had my baby.

When Heath came back with the tea, he sat on the side of my bed. We made no reference to our earlier exchange but it had somehow cleared the air between us. He looked accessible to me.

'I was remembering Joe's birth.'

'It was a shock, I can tell you, when they showed him to me,' Heath said. 'His head was like a marrow. You were white as a ghost, and so weak.'

'And you had no idea what I'd been through. You tried to be jolly and you sent me a bunch of flowers. I felt you were completely foreign, someone I'd never known.'

'I felt the same about you and the baby.'

'I can see why. Men were kept away. It's different now. Roly's probably standing there, holding Rowena's hand if she's had a spinal block, watching with her as they hold up their new baby.'

'He'd faint!'

I laughed too. 'Really, it's much better to include the father. You and I were kept apart. It was the most solitary experience I'd ever known.'

'I'm sorry.'

'Silly, it wasn't your fault. What are we going to do until that damn phone rings?'

'I'll get the crossword puzzle.' He wandered off in his checked dressing gown and old felt slippers; endearingly himself as he combated mental tension with a mental exercise.

When the call came I raced to the phone, not trusting Heath to get the details straight. Roly was relieved and exuberant. I went back to report to Heath.

'The Scarfs have another daughter. And Rowena's fine.'

'Thank God!' said my agnostic. 'How's Roly?'

'Over the moon. They're calling the baby Clarissa.'

'Jolly good. What time is it? Good grief, two a.m.!'

All that shouting, and the Scarfs' crisis, had sprung some shuttered part of my heart. What if our past contained its disappoint-ments? If Heath had seemed to fail me when I needed him, he'd been a victim of a time and place and attitude, just as I had. It wasn't anybody's fault. We needed to get back to the

184

beginning, before I'd let silence and suspicion work their poison in me. The first thing I had to do was to clear away those horrible thoughts about Sophie.

We sat in the quietness of the small hours of morning while I told him about the page of writing. I poured out my worst fears. I finished and fell silent, afraid of his response. But he didn't seem upset with me.

'Did you think the fantasy man was me, Barbie?'

'I didn't know.' I felt ashamed.

'You can put your mind at rest.' He spoke with the usual kindly attitude he always adopted towards our grandchild. 'I know the way some fellows carry on with young girls. Maybe I'm lucky. That's not in my make-up. Things like that have never crossed my mind.'

Through his glasses, his eyes showed such deep concern I knew he was telling the truth.

'I haven't said anything to Sophie.' I pressed his hand.

'What would it achieve? You'd embarrass her. It's obviously fiction. The young generation's different. They know too much, they've heard it all. That's their world. It has to rub off.'

Although he was being realistic, my protest poured out like vomit. 'Why do such terrible things go on? Rape, girls abducted and killed,

185

fathers up on trial for incest? Not even babies in kindergarten are safe today. What's gone wrong, Heath? I can't bear it!'

He held my hand. 'You should have told me. How long has all this been on your mind?'

Tears ran down my cheeks. I couldn't speak but I held on to him as though he was my lifeline. He wasn't guilty. We could be friends again.

★   ★   ★

In the morning we told Sophie the new baby had arrived.

'Cool!' was all she said; but later she offered to help out at the Scarfs' again.

'I don't see why not.' It seemed a good idea to me but, when I put the suggestion to Roly, he was quite off-hand and said he could manage. Tactfully I told Sophie. She went off in a huff to school, leaving me to wonder at the ever-changing moods of adolescence.

I rang the hospital to check on visiting hours and ordered flowers from the three of us. Heath and I stopped by for a very quick visit the next afternoon. Rowena was propped up on pillows, as large as life and none the worse for her emergency that had to do with symptoms of toxaemia. Little Clarissa had the rested, unmarked appearance of an angel plucked straight out of heaven.

On her next visit, my home help wanted to hear all the details of Clarissa's delivery. Being a generous soul, she would arrive next week with some handmade gift for the new baby. But she disapproved of Roly's participation.

'I'd've died if Johnny'd been let in the labour room!' The vacuum cleaner hose slashed my country kitchen chairs like a scythe. 'Birth's not for men.'

'You mean modesty?'

She laughed. 'You can forget that once you're pregnant! A man's just in the way. One more thing to worry about.'

'But they go with their wives to birthing classes now.'

'Don't make me laugh! All the puffun and pantun in the world don't get a baby out no easier.'

'Would you ban male doctors too?'

'Gawd no. Wouldn't want no womun pokun around my insides.'

'Why's that?'

'Well! Men know what they're doun.'

★ ★ ★

If her views were inconsistent, Helen's were plain rejecting. When I said I'd missed seeing

Clarissa's birth, she stared at me in horror.

'What ever did you want to see that for, Mum?'

'Because it's a very special moment, I think.'

Her look said, *I certainly won't be finding out.*

What business was it of mine, if Helen and Alex preferred an ordered life? There'd never been any word about having children. I didn't want to seem nosy. I almost let the moment pass. Helen sensed my thoughts and made sure I was under no misapprehension.

'I won't be having children.'

'Why? You want to keep your figure?'

I meant to sound light but she looked hurt. 'I'm not that shallow.'

How difficult it was to talk to my daughter-in-law! No wonder I always took the easy way out, keeping to surface chat. But I'd had a sharp lesson recently in the damage that attitude could do. So instead I plodded on, knowing I was on risky ground. Helen's response was a deep blush that had nothing to do with her make-up. Her eyes sparkled as though she was on the verge of tears.

'A lot of women don't like babies, Helen.' I meant her to know I was on her side but she stared at me as though I was deranged.

'I *love* babies! It's because I do that I could never face the risks. People lose children all the time. Haven't you read those heartbreaking stories in the magazines? Your baby could be retarded, deformed, premature; *anything*.'

'I realise that.' I spoke carefully. 'Well, even a healthy child's a huge responsibility. Raising Sophie wasn't in our plans, you know. We'd had our family.'

I wanted her to know she wasn't confronting the prospective grandmother, deprived of her doting, but she seemed to think I was complaining.

'Sophie's a *lovely* girl.' She sounded most indignant. I decided to give up on my effort to find rapport with Helen.

'Yes, she is. She's having her sixteenth birthday soon. We'll all have a get-together.'

'Sixteen!' was all Helen said and quite unexpectedly she burst into tears.

'What is it?' I put my arm around her shoulders.

'It's nothing, Mum. Don't worry about it.' Rejecting me, she moved aside, found a perfectly ironed hanky and neatly blew her nose.

'You must be stressed out. Remember, I'm here, if you ever want to talk.' It was all I could offer. Her nod was grateful. But she tucked away the hanky and snapped shut her purse as if to say, *It's my business. I can handle it.*

10

Heath, in his own way, was making quite an effort to improve our relationship. There were flowers from the garden, dinner out at an expensive restaurant, and then the big surprise. With the air of a school-boy presenting a good school report, he handed me a Sydney motel booking and a set of tickets to the opera.

'Do you fancy this?'

I certainly did! The problem was the date of the performance. I put my predicament to Sophie.

'What am I going to do? Darling, it's your birthday weekend.'

She shrugged. 'No sweat, Nan — we can have my birthday any time.'

I had no idea what her accommodating words really meant. Lately she'd slipped away from me. She answered questions and did what she was asked but I felt I didn't know her any more. School uniform couldn't hide her developed figure or her slim legs. Her inner changes were probably as marked. I wished I had Rowena's experience with teenage girls. My boys were somehow more

190

obvious in their behaviour.

'You really wouldn't mind making it a moveable feast this year?'

'No problem. I've got two assignments due, and the music exam. Two days on my own will be excellent.'

'We just want a little time alone . . . '

'Please, Nan, just go! It's fine.'

'Perhaps you could stay at the Scarfs'?'

'I thought Roly didn't want me there.'

'Don't be a silly. He said you did excellent programme notes for his Year 10 concert.'

'I'd rather stay home.'

Heath was penitent when he realised his oversight. He went out and bought her a beautiful leather music case. Joe actually remembered the date and sent a funny birthday card and $20. And Sophie seemed thrilled with my gifts, which I'd have loved at sixteen — perfume, silky underwear and a make-up bag. The night before our Sydney trip, the three of us went out to *Sizzlers* for tea. She didn't want to invite Vanessa.

'She hangs out with the popular people now.'

'But surely you're still friends?'

She just shrugged and I thought how confusing life must be in adolescence.

★ ★ ★

I felt young and open as we headed along the freeway; only a ninety minute run these days to Sydney's approach. Once, we made regular trips to take in a show or concert, but Heath and I hadn't been down for years.

'We'll try the harbour tunnel,' Heath suggested and I was glad to emerge from the enclosed walls into the heart of the city. Ahead glistened the dazzling harbour and shining sails of the Opera House. Heath turned up the hill towards Kings Cross, where two girls who couldn't have been more then thirteen were fooling about with a group of young sailors. A transvestite on platform soles pranced on to the pedestrian crossing, slapped our bonnet and blew us a cheeky kiss.

The motel was past the naval base, in Potts Point. It would be fun to shelve suburbia for a night. Impulsively I reached across and began to stroke Heath's thigh. Suddenly he swung sharp left and parked.

'You're in a five minute zone,' I murmured.

'Then you'd better hurry up.' He smiled at me, leaning back against the headrest.

Once we'd frequented plenty of lonely parking spots. I hadn't felt him, hard like that, for ages, and a twist of desire surprised me. Wolf whistles interrupted us. Heath revved up and drove on but feelings I'd thought gone for good were romping in my body. Kings Cross was as good a place as any to give our married life another chance.

There was off-street parking behind the motel. Arm-in-arm, we checked in, then went for a wander. Ambling groups of tourists moved among the shoppers and street girls. Bottles in hand, a few poor deadbeats shuffled along, their belongings stuffed into plastic bags. Faces one would never see in our sedate suburb stared indifferently. A woman boozing in a doorway glanced at me, her palm cupped. I tried to meet her gaze. At once she looked away. I gave her a few dollars and felt Heath tug my arm.

'Why do that? She'll only buy more grog.'

'I couldn't help it. She had the saddest expression I've ever seen.'

'You're a born touch.' He smiled and squeezed my hand.

* * *

Back in our unit, I lazed in the spa and dressed carefully for dinner. Heath, in his best suit, said he liked my dress and perfume. He'd decided to take a taxi into town. I looked out on The Cross, garish now with strip shows, soliciting and night traffickers. Neon lights flashed raw enticements. What happened to people drawn here by the magnets of quick money and sexual fantasy? We seemed worlds apart. Yet as we sat in our elegant restaurant, picking at prawns with cocktail forks, I knew the same urges ruled transactions everywhere. However packaged, it was sex that drove people to titivate, seek out occasions, smile and touch.

La bohème was an old favourite of ours. Sets and costumes varied with the productions, but the glorious arias endured. After the performance we lingered to read the posters and eye the lights of Luna Park. The tender music had cast its spell and my heart felt open.

'Thank you. I'll always remember tonight.'

Heath smiled. 'Not a bad old show, is it?'

A cab cruised towards us. The moments that impress the mind, becoming memories, may be as small as that one — when Heath raised his arm to hail the driver, and I saw the deep night sky and the stars so sharp I could have counted them, one by one.

We were in no hurry to get going next morning. I lay back in the bath, luxuriating in complimentary bubbles as I tried to figure out the mystery of sex. Our marital life had been restored in that king-sized bed. We'd made love after a fashion, with the help of hand cream and much restraint on Heath's part. A far from passionate encounter, reminding me that the ageing body gets out of practice, yet Heath's step was springy and he was most agreeable. On our way to the Art Gallery I suggested we stroll along the Cross.

'I want to buy some proper lubricant.'

'What — here?'

He sounded shocked and I laughed. 'At least things are out in the open here.'

I was tired of secrecy and suspicion. Heath refused to enter a sex shop but I went ahead, wondering at the extraordinary collection of dildos and devices set out on the counter display cabinets. A young sales girl explained textures, flavours and prices as efficiently as a David Jones' assistant helping with a complexion flaw. Recklessly I pointed to a vibrator.

'I'll have that too.' She began to package the goods. 'Do many women my age come in?'

'What's age got to do with sex?' the matter-of-fact young woman asked. 'I hope you're pleased with these. You've made a good choice.' She handed back my credit card.

Heath almost dragged me to the car. Lurking in the doorway, he'd been propositioned by a girl.

'Weren't you even tempted?' I was joking.

'Don't be so silly! I'm not about to start

violating my marriage vows now.'

We drove on to the Domain. I sat quietly, the parcel on my lap. I knew he was faithful and that he loved me. I just wished he hadn't sounded as though he was wedded to his promises, rather than to me.

★ ★ ★

After that interlude, I turned my mind to work. Recent reading, a memoir of the Australian painter, Stella Bowen, was nudging at my conscience. She was a woman who struggled to paint in spite of her environment. For a long time I'd brushed aside my lack of commitment as a painter. Oh, I'd accepted the portrait commissions and done a workmanlike job, I suppose. But where had the fire of creativity gone? I told myself I was getting older; that Heath and Sophie drained what energy I had. All women artists will vouch for the interruptions that are part and parcel of domestic life. And yet, they learn to cope, they do their work, even as I'm sure they long for the cosseting wistfully voiced by Stella.

To be obliged to tackle other people's problems, or merely to cook their meals, the moment one lays down pen or brush, is intolerably hard. What one wants, on the contrary, is for other people to occupy themselves with one's own moods and requirements; to lie on a sofa and listen to music, and have things brought to one on a tray! That exclamation point says it all.

Yes, Stella, I understand. But I'm not living in a damp and draughty Sussex cottage with mud at the back door, frozen water pipes and a new baby to boot. And my husband is nothing like Ford Madox Ford, who sounds imperious, difficult and impractical. I have Heath, and his good coffee on a tray, and a head full of excuses. So I reminded myself. So was it that I felt I wasn't much good, and that it was safer not to try?

A few weeks of introspection helped me set my course. I dredged from my mind a shelved idea for using watercolour over pastel in a local landscape series. As well, the WEA wanted new tutors. Impulsively I applied to run an evening class there. I was almost done with the portraits. One of the other sitters, a Greek novelist, had taken off overseas before I'd completed the work. She was now back home and we arranged the final sittings. Sylvia Papadopoulas was a pleasure to spend time with. She was unassuming, witty, hard-working. I admired her breadth of experience and felt myself respond to her warm heart. How strange! I knew I wouldn't

197

mind if we never met again. It was Ruth I'd grown attached to.

She had taken a temporary job, cleaning offices.

'You, floor-mopping?' I felt it was such a waste of creative talent.

'It's money, Barbie.'

'But you could run a Creative Writing course. Do some articles.'

'I might think about it.'

I wished she would. The new job made her less available to us. I missed her.

★ ★ ★

I decided to have another dinner party. We were happier at home, and I felt I had established a new direction in my work. A celebration was called for. The Scarfs would be over the initial weeks of managing a newborn baby. I phoned Rowena.

As soon as she heard my voice she spoke abruptly. 'I can't talk now. Sorry, busy with Clarissa.'

And she was gone. It was almost as though she'd hung up on me.

Puzzled, I sat staring at the silent phone. I might have offended her because I hadn't been over for a visit lately. I would pay her an impromptu call. She might need a friend to talk to. One kept one's own problems hidden, imagining everyone else was in top form. I'd never told her about my sexual withdrawal. She and Roly might be going through the self-same crisis; surely, throughout a seventh pregnancy, the last thing on a woman's mind would be sex. Or the baby might be colicky and difficult. I should have seen if she needed any help.

I drove over in Heath's car. Much as I disliked his extravagant choice, I was trying to be less critical. Why shouldn't he have a new vehicle? He'd paid for it after all. I heard him busy with a pupil and slipped out quietly, stopping off to buy a white teddy bear and a tiny smocked dress for Clarissa. I arrived with my gifts and apple teacake just as Rowena was finishing the baby's bath. The expression on her face was most unwelcoming.

'Is this a bad time? I had to see the little pet!'

Rowena soaped fine baby hair with a practised hand. I made baby noises while Clarissa stared at me solemnly.

'No smile for Auntie Barb?'

'She's not recognising faces yet.' Rowena rinsed off soap and scooped the baby into a bath towel. She was avoiding me. There was definitely something wrong here. The whole family had gone into hiding. Roly had had no contact with Heath. Even Vanessa had stopped coming to the house.

The baby's whimpers changed to the rhythmic wail of hunger. Rowena put her to the breast while I stood watching. Usually a nursing mother is a relaxing picture but my friend was cold and unsmiling. The baby gulped steadily.

'Shall I put the kettle on? I've brought a teacake.'

'If you like.'

She must be hurt that I'd shown no active interest in the baby.

'Rowena, sorry I haven't been in touch. I thought you'd want a few weeks' privacy. Is everything OK?'

'Fine.'

'I suppose Vanessa's flat out with assignments, like Sophie?'

'Don't mention Sophie to me, please.'

Her hostility was palpable. I couldn't let it pass. I put Rowena's cup beside her, wondering why she seemed so automatic as she winded the baby and put her to the other breast. Usually she radiated tenderness with a new baby. But depression can strike anybody and she was at a vulnerable age.

'What did you mean, *Don't mention Sophie?* I know there's something wrong. How can I help?'

When she did speak, there was fury in her voice and hatred in her stare.

'Keep that girl away from my family.'

'What are you talking about?' She seemed a little crazy.

'While I was in hospital, she was busy making up to Roly. That weekend you were in Sydney, she lured him to your house and did her level best to make it with him.'

'That's ridiculous!' I almost laughed out loud. Sophie seducing silly old Roly? Poor Rowena was out of her mind. What did they call it? *Puerperal mania* was the old name.

I tried reason. 'Sophie's a child, younger than Vanessa! How could she possibly be interested in Roly?'

How lacking in self-esteem Rowena must be, to make up such nonsense about a teenager. I knew she was suffering and I spoke as gently as I could.

'This is all in your mind. You must see your doctor and get help.'

'I'd like you to go now,' was all she answered. The baby went on sucking, less urgently now. I didn't want to walk away and leave her in this confused state.

'Let me stay. Let's talk about all this.'

'Get out! Don't come here again. I don't want to see you. I don't have anything to say to you or your family.'

I sat in the car, devastated. I'd been in the clutches of suspicion myself, recently. I knew all women had to face the loss of youth and the power it gave us. Well, that was that. I could hardly force her to listen to me. Perhaps I could speak privately to Roly. But, given what Rowena seemed to believe, that would be very awkward. Sophie and Roly? Ludicrous! Yet scenes came back to me. Roly ogling those paintings of satyrs and maidens . . . Sophie obedient as he dropped a sweet into her open mouth . . . That awful page of writing . . .

★ ★ ★

I couldn't go home. I simply wasn't ready to tell Heath about this. Aimlessly I drove to town, parked, and set out to walk along the harbour road. A fresh breeze was blowing off the sea. Reassuring landmarks defined the city I had grown up in. I took comfort from the Anglican cathedral, high on the hill. There was Fort Scratchley on its green hillock, and Nobbys breakwater, its stony finger pointing to the horizon. Mid-harbour, Stockton's dumpy ferryboat slopped its patient way towards the town.

Efforts to dismantle the rail corridor and improve the old buildings were underway.

Restored cottages and public buildings wore new heritage-coloured coats of paint. The Customs House overlooked a wide new brick *piazza*. Transplanted palm trees tossed their shaggy heads in South Seas style, and tarted-up trams stood like girls in a chorus line. The tourist-oriented parade made me feel even more lost. I reached back in my mind to schooldays, biking along ramshackle streets, and student years when we and the Scarfs were young.

The city clock struck one. I hadn't told Heath I was going out. I would simply have to go home and face him. Still upset, I kicked off my shoes and returned along the cold packed sand where Pacific rollers collapsed and fell to froth. The sky was washed-out, hard and pale. The sea wind whirled about me as I scrambled up a dune and headed for the car.

★　★　★

When I did get home, Heath was like an angry parent.

'Where were you? Why didn't you say you were going out?'

I couldn't face an argument. 'Just make me a cup of tea and I'll explain.'

He grumbled, but obliged. I told him what

Rowena had said and waited, hoping for comfort, but Heath was determined to get to the truth.

'I want to know the details. Exactly what did Rowena suggest?'

'Sophie and *Roly*? It's quite ridiculous.'

'It had better be.'

'Where are you going?'

'To get Sophie out of school.'

This felt like those awful scenes during Joe's adolescence. 'Wait! She'll be home soon enough.'

'If this is more than a flight of female fancy, I'm going to the police.' His mouth was set in a thin line of mistrust. In that mood, he wasn't open to reason. What Rowena had said was bad enough. If anything had in fact happened, Heath's anger would only bring worse consequences. There was no mercy in him. He would destroy Roly and his family without compunction.

Fortunately his four o'clock pupil had arrived just as Sophie came in from school. I dreaded questioning her, but better I do it than Heath. Coming straight to the point, I told her what Rowena had implied and asked whether she had seen Roly alone while we were away in Sydney. Expecting to hear her deny everything, I was stunned when she nodded.

'You'd better tell me exactly what happened. And remember, this is very serious.'

★ ★ ★

Sophie said that when Rowena had first gone into hospital, she'd spent time alone with Roly. One night they'd both gone together to collect Vanessa from her cello lesson. They'd waited in the car, chatting in the darkness. There, Roly had confided in her, saying how disillusioned he felt with his life. It was too late for him to fulfil his dreams. All he had was money worries, a ramshackle house, a boring job.

'He really wanted to know what I planned to do with my life, Nan. I shouldn't compromise or go for second best, he said. He seemed to think I was special.'

'Yes. And then?'

'Vanessa came out. We went home.'

She was flattered by his interest. Vanessa was out a fair bit with her new crowd. Sophie didn't like them. They were a wild lot and she felt out of things. Instead, she tried to impress Roly with her competence, storing up his compliments. He gave her fatherly advice, warning her not to be in a hurry to acquire a wedding ring.

'Marriage ruins relationships, he said.'

'A pity about him!' While he spun his hard-luck tale to a school-girl, poor Rowena had been lying in hospital, carrying his child. 'Roly was always weak. He wouldn't face responsibility. He muddled through his degree, roamed around Europe, had to be dragged to the altar and was still making eyes at every woman he saw, even while he was fathering one baby after another.'

My outburst had silenced her. Of course she saw him differently.

'Tell me what happened next.'

'Nothing! We just talked. He said there was no beauty in life, only duty. I felt sorry for him, Nan. And he was nice to me. He paid me compliments. Then Rowena came out of hospital and I came home.'

'I remember you had something on your mind. You seemed withdrawn.'

'Did I? I guess I felt lonely. Vanessa and the group were having a good time. I didn't belong. I kind of missed the way Roly talked. He thought I was beautiful, you know?'

I nodded. I'd been a naïve teenager once. I knew how easy it was to believe persuasive words. She only wanted love.

'But why did Roly come here when we were away? Didn't you think that strange?'

'He had my birthday present. Vanessa had forgotten to drop it over.'

'And I'd asked the Scarfs to look in on you and check you were alright.'

'I offered him a cup of coffee. Well, I was hoping we could have another talk. He helped himself to Granddad's whisky. He kept drinking, talking, raving on and on. Actually, I was getting bored. I think I half went to sleep. When I woke up he was stroking my foot. I laughed. It tickled. He said *You remind me of the Rokeby Venus.* He promised nothing would happen, he just wanted to look at me in the firelight. He undid my blouse. He undressed all my clothes.'

'Sophie, why didn't you stop him, send him home? You knew that was wrong!'

'I didn't know what to do.' Her mouth quivered and I knew she felt ashamed. 'Nan, he'd had a lot to drink. It was almost like I wasn't there. Like I was some dream in his head. It was cold. The fire was nearly out. Then the phone rang. He answered it. Rowena was wondering where he was. He just jumped to and left me there and went off.'

I could tell she'd been humiliated by that casual exit.

'Nan, why did he tell Rowena? It was our secret.'

'Secrets usually come out.' I felt sad for

her. As she'd described things, perhaps she'd come to no great harm. Rowena, waiting alone, had no doubt imagined a far grosser picture. Roly was ever the light-weight. Even in my disgust at his behaviour, I felt compassion that a passing desire could do such damage to us all.

For I knew that would be the outcome. At first Heath wanted to go to the police. I fought to protect Sophie. I knew she'd have to make an intimate statement and submit to cross-examination.

'He didn't force her, Heath.'

'She was one day past fifteen, and he's a man in his forties!'

I wasn't interested in legal loopholes. Sophie was a young girl who had been taught by life's shocks; by a mother who had left her and a father who was seldom present. A heart wounded in that way might do anything for attention and a morsel of love. Yet I couldn't deny a wrong had been done.

'What should we do, Heath?'

Looking old, he sat fingering his beard. 'It was easier, wasn't it, having sons?' was all he said.

11

Persuaded by Alex, the persistent real estate man, and the reality of my dwindling resources, I finally agreed to put the house on the market. The front garden was tidy, though it lacked the artful displays we used to plan and plant together. I had plenty more to do in the back yard. Alex wanted me to cut everything back and cover up the mess with bark. I took no notice, of course. My restoration project had become a mission. I could only leave after the wilderness was under control.

I needed to recreate what Heath and I had carefully built.

The ideal hours to work were early morning, before the heat of the sun drove me inside. I culled mound upon mound of useless over-growth for my obliging handyman to cart away to the tip. So much had gone to waste. I composted what I could, wondering if it would ever find its way back into the earth. The next owner could well be another Alex.

I set myself a task each day — weed the brick path, rake the leaves, dig out the invasive tradescantia and self-sown camphor laurel seedlings. Ferns had gone mad along the back foundations and I spent three full mornings reducing them to orderly clumps. I regretted the arbitrary cutting and chopping, but each day, as I straightened up and pressed my aching back, I was struck by the spaciousness I had restored. Light and air relieved the dense thickets that had crept in and taken over as Heath and I battled more immediate issues.

★   ★   ★

I remember coming back from Sydney with him, both of us buoyed up, hopeful. That was the last time we were happy together. From then on the blows began to fall. The business with Roly was the main factor. Contact with the Scarfs was severed. It was as though our friendship had never been. Trust among the four of us was lost. Poor Sophie felt guilty. Perhaps all young girls taken advantage of by an older man had the feeling they were somehow to blame. She went through a thoroughly bad patch, refusing to sit her music exam or take further lessons. She sat brooding in her bedroom and her marks fell back at school. We never saw Vanessa. Presumably she knew the story and had been

210

forbidden to visit us. Or she may have been taken up with her new circle of friends. If I enquired about her, Sophie's shrugs and monosyllables implied a teenager running wild with an unsuitable crowd.

Heath was moody too. Roly's behaviour had completely shattered him. As well, the money problems must have reached crisis point. If only he'd confided in me! Oh, I'd have nagged, I'd have blamed. But we could have worked out alternatives. It might have been fun, starting afresh in a simpler way. It might have given us a new lease of life. Instead he went about like Scrooge, checking the grocery dockets, switching off lights and turning back the hot water thermostat until we complained of half-cold baths. He made a fuss about the phone bill, especially my long-distance calls to Joe. I had no intention of cutting contact for the sake of a few dollars. A chat with my son cheered me up. So I interrupted Heath's complaints, slapping my money on the table in front of him.

'Don't go on about it. I'll pay!'

He left the money there. I turned and went to do the washing-up. He picked up a tea towel.

'So how is Joe?' Conciliatory words dripped into the silence.

'Fine. Still with Ans.'

'She seemed a level-headed sort of girl. I wouldn't have thought his type.'

'Who can say? Take Alex and Helen — that big wedding, everything done by the book.'

'What about them? They're happy, aren't they? Nice home. Good health. No money worries.'

I upended glasses swathed in detergent rainbows, wondering why appearances satisfied him. Alex and Helen didn't seem happy to me.

He frowned. 'You waste a lot of money on that fancy wash-up stuff. A 2 litre bottle is a quarter of the price.'

His meanness, as I saw it, diminished him in my eyes. Even his appearance seemed smaller. His illness could well have been in its early stages. We didn't know that then, of course.

Sydney, and the closeness that trip renewed, had been all too brief an interlude. My frivolous purchases lay unused in the bedside drawer. At night I went to bed alone while Heath sat hunched over computer spreadsheets. In hindsight it's easy to see how worried he must have been. Nothing was going right for him, financially, healthwise, or in his relationships. Roly had betrayed their friendship. Sophie was a worry to us. I was back to my wrangling, irritable moods. Of course I was shattered too. The pity was that we couldn't share our pain.

Since the row when I'd taken the car without informing him, I was planning to buy a second-hand vehicle myself. I realised that, in relying on Heath to drive me everywhere, I was proving my dependence on him. The issue came up when I was offered the art tutor course at the WEA. The classes would be at night and I would certainly need transport. So I told Heath about the offer. I wondered if he'd mind. In fact, he jumped at the idea.

'Hourly rate or flat fee?'

'I didn't think to ask.'

'You're the most impractical woman!'

'Obviously they'll pay me! I'm thinking, Heath, I might buy a second-hand car.'

'We can't afford to run two vehicles.'

'I could pay for it.'

'What — rego, insurance, repairs, fuel, depreciation costs?'

'But you had your way, when you decided to buy that flashy petrol-guzzler.'

'I'm retired, don't you understand? This is the last decent vehicle we'll own.'

'Heath, don't be silly. We're not paupers.' He seemed to have replaced his talk of ailments with financial shortage lately. I said no more about having a car of my own.

213

Instead I laid my plans quietly. While I saved my pay cheques, I would research brands and costs, and wander on my own in dealers' yards. Meanwhile we solved the transport issue. Heath said he would drive me to my class. He worried about vandals and refused to have the car left parked in town at night. I thought it was a lot of trouble but he wouldn't change his mind.

'Are you sure you want me to accept the job?'

'Of course! Just make sure they pay you the going rate.'

★ ★ ★

Daylight saving began a few weeks after classes started. When we drove to town, it was in the brilliant glare of sunset. I loved everything about my new appointment. The building was an old two-storey place in Union Street. I had about a dozen students who apparently saw me as some sort of expert. They scribbled diligent notes on the basics of the colour wheel and made charts of primary and secondary hues. Most were shy, self-conscious people who looked to me for words of encouragement. I found this quite a new experience, for life at home was tense and I felt my friends had all deserted me. The rift with the Scarfs had an ugly feel of permanence. How unfair it was, when neither Rowena nor I had done anything to cause it. Marian Griffin was on overseas leave with Marcus, and Ruth, of course, was busy at work. I tried phoning her but even then she seemed preoccupied. Her son had failed to answer her recent letters and she felt he must be away on risky army operations. I felt sorry for her. Israeli/Palestinian conflict featured almost nightly on the news. She deferred my lunch invitation as though socialising was too hard to think about.

So my weekly teaching was a relief. The students were a mixed lot. Only a few had any idea of Australian art history. Violet, who was British and sat through my classes with a headmistressy stare, did say she admired the Heidelberg school of painters. She seemed genuinely interested when I brought along examples by Grace Cossington Smith and Margaret Preston. They were other painters from the early 20th century who, like Stella Bowen, persevered to become themselves. I had decided to set aside my excuses and follow them as mentors and examples. The rest of the students must have stuck a pin through the course list. None of them wanted to specialise in portraiture or life drawing. Jack drew cartoons. Mac had a yen for boisterous seascapes. Laura sat frozen, refusing to sully her page with a single pencil stroke, and a Mr. B. Smith, who only attended twice, paid no attention at all to anything I said but made wild swoops and swirls with his fingers, muttering to himself. Simon admired Chinese painting. However my course suited his only free evening. Sally was the class comedian. Her zany animal sketches matched her own outlook on life. The Latrobes were retired. They made a conscious effort to keep the mind young by taking up a new interest every term. They'd done computers, philosophy and line dancing; this was the artistic term. This diverse group soon settled into a surprising camaraderie. People would stand and chat after class, but I hurried away. I felt pressured, knowing Heath was out there waiting, his book tilted towards the dim interior car light.

That situation changed after I had an unexpected phone call from Ruth. She said she'd finished cataloguing Heath's music. Could he collect it some time?

'Of course. I'll tell him.' I guessed she would like to be paid. 'How's life?'

'Busy. Still pushing mops and brooms. But I'm taking your advice and outlining a possible teaching course.'

'That's great! I'm really enjoying mine. Any

news of your son?'

'I've had a letter.' There was an awkward pause; whatever the news, she didn't want to talk about it on the phone. 'When would Heath like to pick up the music? I'm usually home by four o'clock.'

'Perhaps one evening then? He drives me to my class.'

'Lucky lady!' She laughed. I suppose it did sound as though I had a chauffeur at my beck and call. For all that, I was putting away my pay cheques and, when I could, I intended to buy the little car I'd set my heart on.

★　★　★

'Wouldn't it look odd — my going there at night?' Heath seemed uncomfortable at the idea.

'They're her neighbours, not ours! No, of course it won't look odd.'

In fact I was pleased he could pass time with her. He liked Ruth. He was probably as lonely as I was. We were back to a surface relationship. Only recently, he'd put his arms around me and I'd pulled away, letting my disgust at Roly Scarf spill onto him.

'Is that all men can think about? The whole business makes me sick!'

He looked as though I'd slapped his face.

Later I apologised. 'I'm just not myself, Heath. That business with Roly . . . It's done something to me. I can't think about sex at present.'

'Then don't,' was all he said.

★ ★ ★

He seemed pleased with Ruth's work on the music.

'I've lined her up to mend my *Urtext* edition of the Mozart sonatas. Quite frankly, I think she needs the money.'

'Good!' I was happy to think she remained part of our life, even in this small way. 'Was she glad to see you?'

He shrugged. 'She was saying her son has cancelled his visit. Seemed rather down, I thought.'

'She really believed he was coming here to live with her.'

'I'd say she can forget that idea. I gather he's involved with someone.'

'I tried to warn her. What grown man is going to settle for life with mother? It's only natural he'd have a girl.'

'A man,' Heath corrected me. 'I gather Asher's gay. Ruth must have known?'

But I shook my head. 'I don't think she had any idea.'

218

Poor Ruth! No wonder she was so withdrawn. I worried on her behalf. We all cling so to illusions, inventing versions of life to our liking; creating our friends as we need them to be, and our children in our own image of ideal success and happiness. I remembered how differently Heath and I dealt with our disappointment when Joe ran off the rails. At first we were angry, bewildered. And Heath still was. He'd never learned to accept our boy as he was. I felt Ruth had a similar nature to Heath. She had passionate convictions and I was sure that extended to her closest ties. You were with her or against her. I feared she would not forgive Asher for choosing another love.

'Are you calling round to see her next week?'

'I said I'd take the new lot of music over. You don't mind?'

'Of course I don't! Heath, be kind to her.'

'I don't know what you mean, exactly.'

'Let her talk. This news will have upset her. I don't think she has many friends.'

'I can't see any big drama, myself. But yes, I'll let her talk.'

He really didn't understand subtle communication. I let it go.

★ ★ ★

We weren't a cheerful household. Planning my course and reviewing each student's efforts seemed to drain my energy for embarking on a series of my own. On Fridays I pushed the trolley round the supermarket, glad that Heath was busy at the bank instead of counting up every cent we spent. Our little restaurant had closed down. We tried the new place once, but weren't keen on the crowd. Mrs. Looington kept reminding me the year was coming to its close.

'Done your Christmas shoppun yet?'

An amused smile crossed her perspiring face. She knew I hadn't given that a thought. Bargain buys occupied my home help from the first sign of the January sales. She made it a point of honour to wrap and stash her gifts by June. My life seemed to her a series of missed opportunities. Each week she tucked her pay into her large kit and went off on mysterious expeditions, leaving Heath and me to skate about on her wet-mopped floors.

★　★　★

I wondered whether Christmas might bring Sophie and Vanessa back into contact. They had always enjoyed that special time as they helped each other set up lights and decorate their respective trees. My tactful enquiries fell on deaf ears.

'Vanessa goes with the popular people now.'

'Popular people?'

'Ravers. They party, smoke dope, get drunk.'

'Would Vanessa really be so silly?'

Sophie shrugged. She seemed numbed by the consequences of her own mistake. How hard it must be to confront the modern world. The term *teenager* hardly existed when I was at school. We weren't expected to run wild as soon as we reached puberty. I played tennis and netball and gossiped under the gum trees with my circle. The adult world was a closed book to me.

12

I was watching the local news with Heath while we drank our after-dinner coffee. The usual doom and gloom stuff. I wasn't paying much attention. Suddenly I sat bolt upright as the image of a crumpled panel van flashed onto the screen. In the small hours of that morning a car loaded with teenagers had crashed through the guard rail and landed upside down in the lake. There had been two fatalities and several others injured. No names were given out; yet I knew one of those passengers was Vanessa. I stood up and rushed in to Sophie's room.

'Was Vanessa at school today?'

'Didn't see her. Probably wagging.'

Heath always said my psychic flashes were airy-fairy. With all my heart I hoped that he was right. I went to bed uneasy, and had a troubled sleep. The facts came out next day. The news had been given out at school assembly and Sophie came home devastated. Speed and drink had been the key factors in the accident. The driver had got off lightly, but two passengers were dead and one was Vanessa. None of us could eat that evening.

We sat stunned and silent, for what is there to say in the face of such finality? I kept remembering Vanessa as a chubby toddler, then a winsome child who curiously pressed the keys of Heath's piano. She and Sophie had seemed like sisters. The Scarfs had been like an extended family. Now all that was finished. Whatever had happened, no parent should ever have to bear this pain. We could only imagine what Rowena, Roly and their children must be going through but it wasn't possible to offer comfort or support to our old friends. We would be intruding. And knowing that cut me to the heart.

The Death notice was worded in the traditional way. *Scarf. Vanessa Jane. Beloved daughter. Much loved sister. Accidental drowning.* Heath thought we should all go to the service but I refused. It seemed too intrusive. Heath and Sophie did attend, very briefly, while I stayed home alone, sitting on the sun porch, tears streaming down my cheeks as I remembered Vanessa. The subdued knocking of the wind chimes was an echo of sombre bells tolling for that promising young life, cut short.

Ruth phoned a few days later as I was getting ready to travel in to class with Heath. She'd heard the news and offered her sympathy. We spoke for a few minutes, and I suggested we might get together soon for lunch.

'Good idea. My job winds up before the Christmas break.'

Just before we left home, I ran out and impulsively picked gardenias and a handful of the last sweet peas from the browning vines. I hoped Ruth would keep our lunch date soon. I felt sure she needed to talk about Asher. Perhaps my own painfully learned lessons with Joe and Alex could help her to adjust. However different our make-ups, we were both mothers.

'These are for Ruth.' I was wrapping the stems in a twist of wet newspaper as Heath reminded me it was time to leave.

'Is that appropriate?' He sounded uncomfortable and I laughed.

'Every woman loves flowers! If it worries you, say they're from me.'

He had taken to filling in the waiting time at her place. He seemed happy enough with the arrangement although the first few times he'd pointedly brushed dog hairs off his clothing when we got home. Thinking of them poring over the music editions together, I felt less pressured too. Students often approached me after class, wanting a word of private advice.

As we headed along the familiar route to

town, where roof tiles reflected the rich sienna light of dusk, I suggested he ask Ruth to dine with us for Christmas.

'It's a Christian festival. Does she keep it?'

'You could find out. It's a lonely time to be on your own.'

'You mean ask her to the family meal? Will it be the usual?'

'Alex and Helen haven't mentioned their plans. Her parents are a full-time job. She even has to catheterise her father now. It's not right, she's not a nurse.'

'Can't they get community care?'

'Helen won't.'

'Can't be many devoted daughters like that these days.'

'It's not fair to Alex.'

'Not our business though.'

He began the downhill descent. Newcastle harbour, cradled by hills and dunes, was edged by ochre sand. Within minutes we pulled into the car park.

'Hop out.'

He cut the air-conditioning and a rich scent of upholstery, gardenia and sweet pea filled the enclosed space.

'Remember the flowers.'

He laughed. 'If you insist. I'll pick you up around nine thirty then.'

'Happy mending! Don't hurry to be on

time — we like to chat, after class.'

Heath tooted and drove away. I walked into the foyer. There, students and teachers milled around, their access to the rooms blocked by two policemen. Violet waved. I went over to her.

'What's going on?'

'They're in no hurry to enlighten us. A break-in, I gather.'

'Are we banned from classes?'

A tough-looking cop signalled us away. The younger policeman was more polite. Classes were cancelled; would we please leave the premises. Outside, students from my group wanted to know what had happened. A disconsolate gathering, we stood in the car park.

'Right-oh, folks!' Violet swivelled like a sergeant major. 'This is no jolly good, everybody round to my place for drinks!'

I'd come to like Violet, who took diligent notes and had tried her hand at all the exercises I suggested. The unnerving stare, I'd learned, was the result of a whiplash injury. She said her unit was only five minutes' walk away. A few people declined her offer and the elderly Latrobes said they would drive. I joined the others, wandering along Laman Street where geraniums filled window boxes and music drifted from the barred windows of terrace houses. The doors of the conservatorium recital hall stood open for some concert.

'How do you like Newcastle?' I asked Violet, as she marched us past the Presbyterian church, library and art gallery.

'It's hardly London. It's not too bad.'

Her nostalgia reminded me of Ruth's tone whenever she described Israel. However far a migrant travelled, she must always feel that tug.

★ ★ ★

Violet's unit overlooked the city and harbour. She offered sherry or Earl Grey tea, bringing out bone china teacups apparently reserved for visitors. Art was the common thread of conversation and the feedback on my classes was encouraging. Some of the group asked about a follow-up course. We discussed possibilities — pastels, acrylics, a general drawing course. I was happy to be in demand, yet it was clear to me that teaching absorbed the energy I needed for concentrated work of my own. So I said I'd think about it, knowing that their words came from appreciation and would very likely be forgotten in the general press of busy lives.

The disrupted evening had turned out well

after all. By eight-thirty most people had wandered off. I was just planning to phone Ruth's and explain the change of plan to Heath, when the Latrobes said they were driving home in that direction. I accepted their offer of a lift to Ruth's. Heath's car was parked outside. As I walked up to the house I could hear the out-of-tune piano and the dog, barking from the back yard. The front door was ajar, and the screen door unlocked. I walked along the hall and stopped dead in the lounge room, stunned by what I saw.

Heath was at the piano, hamming up some old sheet music ballad. Ruth stood beside him, her arm resting affectionately around his shoulders. He was in fine form, singing loudly. *The right thing to sa-ay, isn't easy to sa-ay*, as he added such a florid cadenza that Ruth burst out laughing. She moved closer, her cheek against his as she bent to read the lyrics of the stupid song. I saw the empty champagne bottle, the glasses, the candles flickering in the menorah. They illuminated the vase of sweet peas I had sent her.

The last chords crashed out. Sensing my presence, they both turned round, startled. I felt the surge of rage and jealousy. Here was a happy man, joking, laughing, playing along with an attractive woman who had her arm around him and her cheek pressed to his.

Their unselfconscious intimacy made me want to cry.

I hid behind sarcasm. 'Do excuse me, I should have knocked.'

I refused to speak about it to Heath until we arrived home. Then our fight was short and savage. Heath denied everything. I paid no attention to his excuses.

'When did you decide to have an affair with Ruth?'

'I'm not having an affair with Ruth! We were playing the piano!'

'Oh yes? Wine? Candles?'

'They were her idea. She wanted to celebrate.'

'Celebrate what?'

'I don't know. How would I know what a woman means when she says, Let's have a celebration?'

'I think you know quite well.'

'You're twisting the facts. So I was laughing, I was enjoying myself. Is it a crime? There's not much laughter in this house.'

'Blame me now?'

'God almighty! Are you paranoid? I'm not having any bloody affair. You know I've never been unfaithful.'

'So you keep saying.' I stormed out.

★　★　★

That all took place a year ago. November was dry, the garden wilted, we had to water night and morning. After a fashion, we patched things up. It had been one of those years. The next one was bound to be better.

★ ★ ★

Not so, of course. The snapshots my mind recorded seemed to fasten on scenes of shock and pain.

I'm kneeling, weeding the petunias as Heath walks up the path. He's been tired, unwell, and he's been down to the doctor to pick up his test results. He stands gazing down at me.

The Christmas lilies are in bud, I tell him.

He looks gravely into my face. *Barbie, I've got cancer.*

★ ★ ★

Helen brings in the turkey. Alex carves. Lunch is at their house this year. Heath and I pull our Christmas crackers and don our coloured party hats. Glasses clink together. Around the table I see three tense, sorrowful faces. No doubt I look the same to them.

★ ★ ★

The Department of Nuclear Medicine is a setting from an old *Star Trek* show. Squat, shiny machines from a technological future wait to process Heath. Robotic arms glide forward to receive him. Gowned figures come and go. I don't understand their language, nor they mine. They are from Krypton.

★ ★ ★

Sophie and I walk beside the lake. We come to a small white cross, fixed to the repaired guard rail. Beneath it, like household goods in a Pharaoh's tomb, lie a cushion, a pair of Doc Martens boots and a jacket. The fabrics have faded and the boots are dull. They have been lying out in the weather for months. Nobody has touched them. They are talismans of doom. Sophie points to the jacket. *That was Vanessa's.* We leave our flowers there.

★ ★ ★

Do you love me, Barbie? Heath's grasp is pitiful. I don't want to hold his hand. It's all I can do, not to shake off that feeble claw demanding my love. *Of course I do.* I have spoken automatically for I have no idea what I feel. He seems to accept my words. He

231

sighs, closes his eyes, relieved. The morphine is taking effect.

* * *

Ruth is at the funeral. At one point, when I think she's coming over to me, I quickly address myself to one of Heath's colleagues. Next time I look, she has disappeared. I shiver in the bitter graveside wind. We turn away; a little procession, making for the car park.

* * *

One forlorn potato bubbles in the pot. One lamb chop lies lonely on the griller. Soon I wash up my few dishes and switch on the ABC. The day's events don't seem interesting. I turn the sound off. Images flicker silently — a kind of company. I can't run a bath and go to bed at a quarter past six. The sky's not even dark. How matter-of-fact death is! I map this past, recognising it is of no significance to anyone except myself. The facts tell it all. Heath fell ill and passed away. Vanessa Scarf lived out her seventeen years and then she died.

13

I made lists of things to do prior to moving house. My thoughts had shifted to practical mode, spurred on by the agent's visits with potential buyers, my home help's demands that I clear out drawers and cupboards, and my own exertions in the garden. I could be out of my home by Christmas. Banksia Grove was substantially developing but I knew I wasn't interested. Once the sale took place, I might rent a place while I figured out finances and options. Sorting and clearing stirred up plenty of memories and I became ruthless in disposing of goods. I wouldn't need a quarter of the possessions Heath and I had gathered. At times, thinking of the new life ahead, I felt the stirring of excitement.

But my equilibrium was shaken when I found two letters in my mailbox. Sophie's news was a delight. She sounded very happy but reminded me I'd promised to pay them a visit in Bingara. It was the sealed letter from Ruth that caused my hand to shake. The last thing I wanted was to be drawn back into the past with its horrible suspicions, doubts and sorrows. I hadn't acknowledged the card she'd sent, but a letter was harder to dismiss.

Can't we meet? Seems I may be taking a job in Sydney in the New Year. It would be good to clear the air, don't you think? I'd like to see you, if you're willing. Thinking of you, Barb — Ruth.

Standing there in the warm sunshine, rereading the few words, I felt an overwhelming desire to escape the past. Perhaps I'd been hoping for just such an offer; now I simply wasn't ready to deal with it. I gazed at Sophie's envelope, with its bows and hearts and kisses. I would go and visit her. Surprising, how quickly you can dismantle a life and delegate responsibility. A few quick calls to the estate agent, my sons and Mrs. L. and a few clothes in a suitcase — and early next morning I was driving Heath's car north along the New England route. Any worries that I'd get lost were soon put to rest. Surely none but the blind could have difficulty in finding Bingara. White arrows steered me right or left. Green, blue and brown roadside signs helpfully reported on destinations, information centres and historic interest sites. Beyond the city boundaries, I eased into the mindset of a long-distance traveller.

The drought was over and the countryside was green again. Venetian red foliage tipped the regenerating bush. Grazing cattle were sleek. Rain had topped up the drinking holes and creek beds. I was passing through townships Heath and I used to visit, but I had no time now to browse. I had my own way to find and a long way to go. Slag heaps, silos, and power grid towers flashed by. Branxton. Aberdeen. Scone. Murrurundi. These towns were landscape sketches, each corner-site hotel adorned with old-fashioned iron veranda lace and generous balconies. A Mechanics' Institute, Masonic Lodge, a church or two, a bowling club and the all-purpose store. Wooden cottages crouched under towering Corot skies. Curled into the flanks of the Great Dividing Range, farm-houses were hazed in blue-violet light. Here and there along the intervening miles, ancient fruit trees raised clawed branches entangled in creepers. On the road, slain roos and foxes lay slumped or splattered, ravens running the gauntlet for their feast.

Bypassing Tamworth I kept the speedo at 100 km until Manilla, where I filled up on gas and used the restroom before pressing on. Along the Fossickers' Way, a school bus or farm gates were events. This lonely mining country had attracted my own father, along with thousands seeking a living from the elusive treasure in the ground. Men would have ridden or trudged along dirt tracks, hoping to beat the odds of poverty and unemployment. By then, the first rush was already over. My dad sometimes spoke about those times. He was a dreaming man. When he talked, he left out the reality of greed and counter-claims and kangaroo court justice. He told of crystals, sapphires, opals, gold. The caskets of my fairy tales spilled over with his images of jasper, garnet and topaz jewels.

Later I learned that men had paid a high price for those dreams. The landscape was gentle now. It stretched away in pale tussock daubed with trembling stands of grey-green gum trees. This same ground was once sodden with racial hatreds, fights and murders. The ranges rose up ragged, as though a maniac had run along the horizon with a cosmic chainsaw. My dad came home empty-handed to my mother. I recognised the silent disappointment in her manner but never understood its cause. Who knew what she'd coped with, battling on alone? Those days were only hearsay. I was not yet born. Children can only pick up on an atmosphere to create their own futures.

Barraba was no more than a loop in the road. I was tired now. The cloud-shrouded hills were pink and the river was gilded as I came to Bingara and fumbled for my scribbled instructions. The screech of sulphur-crested cockatoos echoed from the cedar forests. The house was just a little further, on a side road out of town. Feeling my age, I disentangled myself from the seat belt and climbed stiffly out. They had been watching for me. Sophie hugged me, then I was in the crush of Joe's arms. I could never decide if I liked such ardour, but how good it was to see them both!

Ans hung back, her little girl in tow. I hoped she didn't mind my coming. Here I was, a second female invading her love nest. Sophie went ahead, her father's arm clasped in ownership. I followed, ducking the Naples yellow arches of an old banksia rose. Their yard was a child's paradise, with a rope swing and trampoline, trees begging to be climbed and a free-range nanny goat and chickens.

'Are you Nan?' The child skipped along beside me.

'Indeed I am.'

'Would you like to see my tree house?'

'Tomorrow, Hedda!' Ans turned to me, her smile warm and welcoming. 'You must be tired. I don't suppose you've eaten?'

'Only a few sandwiches in Manilla.'

'Homemade soup?'

'Sounds good.'

An aroma of steaming vegetables and baked bread greeted me. It was a single room we entered, the furniture roughly defining kitchen, dining and sitting areas. A dinner place had been laid for me, complete with daisy chain and wildflowers. Hedda seated herself beside me, observing as I began to eat.

Joe settled back, long legs stretched out and dirty work boots propped on the sofa arm. There was no such person as the social Joe; he'd gone to no ceremony on my account. I would never forget the sleepless nights Heath and I had spent, arguing about our problem son. Poor Alex didn't get a look-in as his brother's escapades consumed all our energies. As Heath grew angrier, I clung to memories of a little boy who gently stroked a day-old chick; who slept trustingly, his flushed face damp with earnest dreams. Those images were all I had to offset the grown Joe; images chipped and damaged, but, like precious heirlooms, too valuable to ever throw away.

Sophie sat on the floor, her head resting against his leg. Joe's benevolent expression reminded me of David Attenborough observing from his hide the territorial behaviour of the animals. *Love me, love my lifestyle.* I watched the pair affectionately, my smile becoming a yawn that nearly dislocated my jaw. Hedda considered me gravely.

'You are much older than my mother.'

'Yes, I am.'

'Are you Sophie's mother?'

'Joe's mother.'

'He's too old to have a mother.'

'No. Everybody has one.' I yawned again and Ans smiled at me.

'You must be dead! Why don't I show you the bedroom?'

She led the way to a small annexe with uncurtained windows.

'I'll give you a sheet to hang there. Joe and I like to lie and look out at the stars.'

So they'd given up their own room. She brushed aside my apologies.

'It's fun camping out, even if it's only on the lounge-room floor. Here's the bathroom. There's only a basin to wash in. Joe's pulled out the bath to fix the leaks. Can you work these old water heaters? I'll show you.' She struck a match and demonstrated. Hedda was observing everything.

'Which story will we read tonight, Nan?'

'Tomorrow, Hedda! Don't bother Joe's mother now. She's been driving a long, long way.'

I smiled at the little girl. 'You can call me Barbie, if you like. Bring your story books and show me in the morning.'

'Shall we hang that sheet?' asked Ans. We stood together, assessing the midnight-blue sky. Its colour reminded me of tiny Evening in Paris scent bottles I used to buy as a girl.

'I think I'll just enjoy the view, like you. I expect no peeping Toms will be about.'

'We'll just let you get settled then. There's tea and coffee in the kitchen, if you want.'

'Happy dreams, Barbie!' chanted Hedda as she was led away by Ans. There was no doubt about my welcome here.

★ ★ ★

I hadn't realised how chilly a warm country day could turn. Shivering, I closed the window. There was one old quilt spread on the bed. Extra visitors must have stretched resources very thin but fortunately I'd packed a tracksuit. As I finished changing, Sophie wandered in to chat.

'Darling Nan. Thanks for coming. I've missed you a lot! How's it been at home?'

She meant, without Heath. Briefly I explained why I had to sell up, and tried to ease her worries. 'The house is too big, anyway. We won't be destitute. There'll be enough to get by on. We'll just live a simpler life.'

I was making it clear there would always be room for Sophie.

She hesitated. 'I might stay on here for a while.'

'What does Ans think of that idea?'

'She's cool. So's Dad. And the local school's fine.'

The bed let out an alarming groan as she bounced down on the mattress.

'Should hear it go sometimes in the night!' She giggled. It was good to see she was back to her older, cheerful self. She deserved answers to the life-long puzzle of her parents and, now she'd tracked Joe to ground, I could understand her need to stay. I reached over to kiss her cheek.

'Joe and Ans seem to get on well. Let's see how they both feel about you staying on, before you make too many plans.'

After she'd wandered off, I stood at the window, contemplating the abstract painting in night's gallery. Uneven ridge caps traced a meandering divide, Prussian blue above, black below. Somewhere a dog barked and a night bird called.

* * *

In the morning Hedda arrived with picture books and I read to her as promised. After breakfast she conducted me on a tour of the yard, showing me the various projects underway — the bath, the compost heap, the veggie patch, the half-laid crazy paving path.

241

Solemnly she showed me the hen house, the beehive and the nesting boxes. To reach her *pièce de résistance*, the tree house, I had to negotiate plastic chairs, pipes and sheets of iron. Hedda shinned up the short rope ladder and waved from the timber platform. I was to learn that this was where she liked to retreat when Ans had friends over. There was a social life busier than I would have expected in this tiny country town. Babies came stashed in backpacks and slings. Toddlers explored, shrieking when mothers interrupted to wipe runny noses and unbutton dungarees. In those warm spring days I often wandered off alone. Time expanded on those walks. Past and future dimmed to a mirage of passing endeavour. My interest focused on the vermilion and emerald-green of squabbling parrots and the galahs shocked into rosy flight from their ground-level hides. The angle of a leaning gate was enough to stir the urge to sketch.

I was part of a family again. At night I slept soundly. I did justice to Ans' hearty meals. Joe came and went in his ancient truck, intent on missions to do with hardware and timber. Sophie read and sunned herself. Ans dug and planted and cooked up appetising vegetable pies and stews. There was very little talk about money, though I knew the budget must be tight. They reminded me of the Scarfs when they were both young and carefree. Everything here might be old and threadbare but there was no shortage of food. Hedda had toys, Joe could rustle up the cash for hardware and Ans for her seedlings. Diffidently (one didn't shop for Helen without a consultation) I bought a pretty bed quilt and a set of paints for Hedda when we took a run into the township, and was glad when my gifts were welcomed with no fuss.

After a week of warm days and winds that shook the cottage, summer arrived. The temperatures soared into the 30s. Without even a fan, I couldn't sleep. On those balmy, sticky nights I would sit out on the porch under Van Gogh whorls of stars. My light clothes were at home. Ans lent me a Hawaiian wrap-around and Joe spotted me lazing with Sophie in the shade, hens pecking at my feet, hibiscus flowering on my hip. He grinned and pulled me to my feet, grinding his pelvis and flapping his thighs in a mock *tamore*.

'How's my *wahine* from Papeete?'

'Enough! I'm hot.'

Sophie didn't miss her chance. 'Dad! Tell us how you met Mum in Tahiti.'

He ruffled her hair. 'I was there with the band. We did this concert at a leper colony.

They started touching us, getting us to sign autographs. Man! That freaked me. I went down the beach to sterilise myself in the sea and there's this pretty girl, shiny white swimsuit, big round moon . . . '

'Did you fall in love?'

'Heck, your mum was a looker. I wasn't bad myself. We just wanted a good time. She'd watch our show and then we'd hang out. It was a holiday fling.'

'Only Mum got pregnant with me?'

'I'd been back in Newcastle a couple of months and Julie turns up. 'You better marry me,' she says, ' 'cos we're having a kid.''

'I remember that day quite well,' I confirmed. 'This slip of a girl arrives at my front door, determined to track down Joe.'

'How did you feel about it, Dad?'

'Hell, Julie was all right. You were cute.'

'But why did she leave?'

'I was always on the road. She got bored. And she thought I was playing around.'

'She just went off and left me behind.'

'Honey, say it was you with a kid, no job, no money. See, we weren't a whole lot older than you. We were kids ourselves. I'm not making excuses. I guess she was just unhappy.'

'But where is she now?'

Joe was clearly restless. 'Pick my brains

about something else. How about Tahitian drumming?' He beat out a tattoo on her back as she squealed and fought back. 'That's lesson one. I'm going in to town now. See ya.'

As he drove away, Sophie was still thoughtful.

'He doesn't hate Mum, does he?'

'He doesn't bear grudges. Live and learn, that's his motto.'

She nodded. 'Have you asked Ans yet about my staying on?'

'Are you quite sure about this?'

She nodded. 'Will you talk to her and Dad?'

'I can do that, I suppose.'

* * *

I had an opportunity later that day. Joe had taken the girls to the local pool, but neither Ans nor I could face the blazing sun. Armed with insect repellent, hats and a flask of iced lemon drink, we waded through long grass to a grove of trees beside the river. We sat on the bank, cooling our feet in the water. I glanced at her profile. Calm and self-possessed, she might have gazed out from a Victorian picture-frame.

'How long have you lived in Bingara?'

245

'I grew up here. Went off to Melbourne for six or seven years, in my twenties, then came back.'

'A country girl at heart?'

'Cities aren't my scene.'

'How did you meet Joe?'

'Just passing through.' She didn't elaborate. I nodded, realising one rarely plans the significant encounters of life.

'You two seem to get along well.'

'So far!' She was old enough that she left room for caution.

I wondered about Hedda's father and she seemed to pick up on my thoughts.

'Joe's good with Hedda. Her Dad took off when she was just a baby.'

'Hard on you?'

She shrugged. 'At the time. You can't waste life feeling sorry for yourself.'

Like Joe, she had an easy way of releasing the past. I decided to tell her some of my granddaughter's background.

'Joe missed Sophie's childhood, you know.'

'The job fell to you. I think you and your husband did pretty well.'

'Thank you. It certainly wasn't planned, but she's brought a lot of joy.'

'You're wanting to ask if she can stay on here, I think?'

I nodded, thinking Joe's former glamour

pusses would never have shared him with a daughter.

'She has the idea she wants to do her last school year up here.'

'A chance of solid time with her father before she strikes out on her own. Why not?'

'More work for you; more expense?'

'Sophie's welcome to share what we have.'

We sat quietly after that, drinking in the peace of those simple surroundings.

14

I felt no anticipation about going home. As I reached Newcastle's outskirts and approached my suburb, I observed the gases smoking from Pasminco, and the barren surfaces of quarried hills. I paused to buy bread and milk, then followed the lake road, stopping in a parking bay near where Vanessa Scarf had died. Since the accident I'd only been to the site once. Sophie went there often. I suppose she grieved that her friend had gone with no chance ever to make peace. I wished I'd given her more support. At the time, Vanessa's tragedy was just one more link in my own chain of loss.

I stood looking at the white wooden crosses nailed to the repaired guard rail. It was all too easy to imagine teenagers screaming as their vehicle slewed across the road and plunged into the lake. The personal salvage items were gone. I hoped the families had taken them. A posy had been laid very recently. There was something reassuring in those symbols. Crosses and flowers reminded me of the way my children learned of death, burying a mouse in a matchbox.

An evening breeze ruffled the lake's surface and I shivered as a memory returned. I was beside Heath's open grave, and my feelings were bitter and resentful. I didn't need those feelings now. I thought of Roly and Rowena and wondered when they made their pilgrimage. They would choose a peaceful time, early morning or dusk, to bring their offering and stand remembering their daughter. Their faces appeared in my mind's eye and I had an urge to see them again. I would make the first move soon.

At home, the blunt *For Sale* sign jarred me into the present. As I surveyed the shed, all I could see was work to do. I'd have to organise a garage sale and hurry along my efforts to clear the back garden. The house smelt stale. The agent's calling cards were scattered on the table. Strangers had walked through my home. Soon someone would buy it. I might not have much time left.

The full force of change was frightening. I began to imagine all kinds of bad scenarios. Bailiffs and debt collectors would come knocking. I'd end up dependent on my children, stuck in a tiny bedroom, apologising because I was alive. The first few nights back home, I felt uneasy as a child convinced a monster lives under the bed. The smallest setback, a spilt vase or stubbed toe, set me off in gusts of tears. Perhaps this was the fashionable condition of *stress*. It felt horrible.

When I rang Alex to say I was back, Helen answered the phone. She sounded pleased to hear from me and I invited her over to lunch. When she arrived, her appearance shocked me. In the space of a few weeks she'd become haggard. Impulsively I gave her a hug. Rather to my surprise, she kissed my cheek and asked how the trip had gone.

'Extremely well. Sophie's happy. In fact she's going to stay on with them.'

'I missed you, Mum. It's a shock, that *For Sale* sign outside.'

'I can't put it off. My money's almost gone.'

'Where will you go?'

I shrugged away her question but she saw through my act and repeated her offer to have me stay with them. Instead of shying away, I felt grateful. Perhaps I was more in touch with my predicament; or perhaps her gaunt face reflected some crisis that made us equals. As she sat picking at her food I could see how troubled she was.

'How are your parents?' I enquired. At once she opened up. Her mother had fallen and broken her femur. The old lady was in hospital and Helen's father had been placed in respite care. Helen was devastated.

I was puzzled. Surely she must know that all the love in the world couldn't hold back the relentless changes of old age? Of course there were ethnic values I didn't share.

'I'm so unhappy, Mum!' Tears set mascara streaks running down her smooth cheeks.

'What's happened? Is it trouble between you and Alex?'

'It's not that. In fact, we're getting along much better. Mum, I'm pregnant.'

'That's wonderful!'

Helen only began to cry more. I reached over and put my hand on hers.

'You really don't want to have a baby?'

'I just can't forget what happened. It's all come back to me. I had an abortion when I was seventeen. I met the man at my first job. He was married. So stupid. What does a girl of that age know? He said he loved me.'

There was the self-same cry I'd heard from Sophie about Roly.

'That was a long time ago,' I suggested gently.

'It had to be done in Sydney. He arranged things. I couldn't tell my parents. There was no help, no counselling. You went there, you got it over. The money was paid. You were supposed to be grateful. Someone had got you out of a hole.'

She had a faraway expression. 'Haven't you ever wondered why I didn't want children?' I nodded. 'Now you know.'

'Some medical problem?' I knew mismanaged abortion could have lifelong repercussions.

She shook her head. 'I didn't think it through. I didn't know anything. It didn't occur to me till I was on the table that this was different from having my teeth drilled. Then, months later, I began to notice girls wheeling prams and pushchairs.'

'No one to help you? No one to talk to?' I could imagine her sense of loss behind that bright, efficient mask.

'The romance was over. I didn't see him after that. I was an issue. He couldn't be bothered. I tried to forget it all. I still lived at home. I got another job. But odd things began to happen. I'd go into op.shops, buy toys and baby jackets, hide them in my room. I'd count up the months and have a little ceremony; you know, for the baby's birthday, when she walked and talked and started school. She'd be Sophie's age now.'

'You thought it was a girl?'

'Yes. That's what I decided. It didn't work, convincing myself I'd got rid of a bloody mess, like a bad period. That's not what my church taught. I still don't know. Mum, was it a baby? What do you believe?'

I handed her a tissue. I was shocked to think my daughter-in-law had been carrying this burden alone. 'I don't think beliefs help much when you're suffering.'

'But was I right or wrong?'

'Helen dear! All you know for sure is, this happened. It was one of the options but none of them were all that great. You might have been a teenage mother, battling alone. Today, yes, you might have a grown son or daughter. Or you might have miscarried or lost the baby. Who knows? It's past and gone. Is this why you're clinging to your parents, far beyond the call of duty?'

'How can I abandon them?'

'I know you feel that way. Haven't you ever discussed all this with Alex?'

'You're the first person I've told.'

'In seventeen years!' This poor, broken girl was so unlike the armoured person I was used to.

'Alex and I respected the other's past. Didn't ask questions. It wasn't his problem.'

'Except that it's still affecting you.'

'Especially now I'm pregnant. I'm so frightened something will go wrong. I couldn't face it — well, it happens, Mum. SIDS. Horrible diseases. The trauma of growing up. Think about Vanessa Scarf.'

'I know. You're afraid, so you made Alex think you didn't want to lose your figure or the house would be a mess? Alex might be kinder if you're honest.'

'I'm not sure. He can be judging.'

Like his father. 'Don't let him be! Fight him, make him understand. He will if he loves you.' I sighed. It wasn't my son's forgiveness she needed, but her own.

'I don't have much choice now, do I?' She managed a smile.

'It's hard, isn't it? We're lonely if we don't speak out. And if we open our hearts, we risk rejection.' I gave her another tissue and she blew her nose.

'Thanks for listening,' she said.

*　*　*

I was a passenger in a transit lounge. The agent continued to bring prospective buyers, often at short notice. He was a hard-working fellow who handled queries like shrewd line balls. Each time he left, his glance carried a *you'll be hearing from me* message. Most unsettling.

Every week I had dinner with Alex and Helen. Although my daughter-in-law had resumed her normal manner, I sensed a change between us. I never referred to that painful confession but I saw her very differently. Her passionate protection of her parents was her way of nurturing the child she'd abandoned; for that was how her heart judged that clinical experience. She'd been the victim of youth, with its childish wish to obey and please. At the mercy of a man with power and money, how could she possibly have foreseen her psyche's revenge? Her unborn child would go on dying a thousand deaths, in all the sad ways a real child could die. I could only hope the telling of her past would be healing, and that child-bearing and parenthood would bring both her and Alex close.

Objects vary according to the light cast on them and the same can be said of the events that form our lives The past year had taught me how I'd judged Heath's gambling, Roly's lust, Helen's coldness and Ruth's betrayal of my friendship. But loneliness and solitude cast different shadows. Surely we'd all colluded? Rowena had substituted her family for Roly and then refused to face his escapist weakness. Alex had been too wrapped up in his own world to want Helen's truth. Sophie had given in to sexual curiosity and her hungry need for love.

As for my own role in the drama, I'd had Heath so neatly packaged it was no wonder he couldn't let me see his failures. He gambling on our security rather than admit his mistakes. Instead, he confided in Ruth. In return, she shared her disappointment over Asher. In her company, he remembered he was a man who laughed and liked feminine attention. Ruth was the perfect candidate to give it. She'd never hidden from me that she liked Heath. I hadn't bothered to take her seriously, or was too arrogant to imagine Heath would ever stray, even in his thoughts.

But I was lucky. I had a chance to repair my life. Poor Heath was dead and the Scarfs had lost a daughter. Roly and Rowena had to live with that pilgrimage to a small white cross beside the lake.

★　★　★

I thought of Ruth when I turned on the news and heard about the assassination of the Israeli Prime Minister, Yitzhak Rabin. He'd been shot at close range, ironically at the biggest peace rally seen in Tel Aviv for years. I knew almost nothing about him. They said he'd once headed the army, been transformed into a peace advocate and won a Nobel peace prize. There were pictures of an elderly, bespectacled man in a suit and tie, speaking into a microphone minutes before his death. They'd tracked down replays of his voice, delivering his message. *Peace you do with enemies. With friends, there is no need to make peace.*

The next few days I slept uneasily. Thunderstorms rumbled on for hours. On their heels came a southerly. Windows rattled and the wind chimes clanked. The assassination continued to dominate the news. Diplomats and writers on the Middle East put forward their interpretation of events. The screen showed Tel Aviv and Jerusalem crowds, stunned and weeping. There was a particular horror for them, learning a Jew had carried out the act. Nations, like individual families, believed their own members were exempt from evil acts.

★   ★   ★

I thought about Ruth constantly. She'd be gleaning every scrap of news from radio and TV — alone. As she watched the solidarity of those mourning crowds, only the stray dog would be there to share her feelings. Hebrew speech filled our living rooms and Hebrew captions flashed over the news scenes. How she must be longing for fellowship. Yitzhak Rabin hadn't grown up in an English-speaking home as she had, but they were citizens of the same nation, who'd fought for a common cause. He'd been the David who, on the very day of her birth, had led his army through the Six-Day War to triumph over the Goliath Arab nations. It wasn't until much later that he'd been transformed. Replays of his words conveyed the sober understanding of a man who'd tried both courses. I kept thinking of his comment about making peace with enemies. I'd felt absolutely justified in rejecting Ruth. But she wasn't my enemy. I knew I had to speak to her.

Next morning I phoned her. She sounded tired. It was hard to gauge her mood. I asked how the news was affecting her.

'It's shocking.'

But she seemed less upset than I'd expected. Of course she'd seen many brutal acts and vengeful reprisals. Perhaps she'd wearied of violence, even as Rabin had done.

'And how are you?' she enquired.

I said the house was up for sale. I had no doubt Heath had confided his financial worries to her. 'I was thinking we could meet and talk.'

'Why not? Did you get my note?'

'Just as I was on my way north to visit Joe.'

'I'm free tomorrow. Does that suit?'

'Come for coffee.'

'Ten o'clock then.'

The conversation had been brief and quite formal but I felt relieved.

★   ★   ★

I thought she looked older. We walked down the hall, past Heath's studio with its closed piano fall, and into the kitchen. My former sense of pleasure and excitement had quite gone. I used to look forward so keenly to her visits. She seemed then to have some power to extend me and make me wish I'd lived a fuller, braver life. Objectively I saw someone whose accumulated deeds and thoughts were written into the severe lines of her face. Other faded threads I'd never noticed matched the dramatic white streak in her dark hair. I went to pour the coffee, glad of a task while I assessed my feelings.

'I've had a job offer in Sydney,' she said. 'I'm taking a flat in Darlinghurst, near the Jewish community. I'll be connected with the Holocaust Museum.'

'What sort of work?'

She laughed. 'Archival. Pen-pushing. Make a change from a mop!'

'You'll be writing? I'm really pleased. A new beginning for you.'

'Yes. And you're moving? Will you stay in Newcastle?'

'I think so. Alex and Helen are expecting.'

Again I felt awkward. On the topic of our sons, she used to speak so possessively about Asher. But now she was silent. I'd lain awake the night before, rehearsing conversations I might have with Ruth.

— *Didn't you feel guilty, Ruth, making up to Heath when you and I were friends?*

— *Barb, I was open with you, that day you came to lunch. I didn't hide my feelings. I thought you understood. You didn't seem to mind. Did I get the wrong end of the stick?*

— *I had no idea you meant to go so far . . .*

— *Must we dissect the past like this? He was terribly hurt, you know, the way you cut off intimacy.*

— *I thought you'd know all about that. I had my reasons.*

— *I think we should forget it.*

But now I couldn't talk about Heath, any more than she wanted to open up about Asher. The closeness between us was no longer there. Perhaps she'd never felt it. Her talent and her flamboyant life had dazzled me, but perhaps I had merely stood for security and a domestic life. Now, I didn't care about her past. The magic aura had gone. She was the mirror Heath and I had looked into, to see our own deficiencies.

So when she smiled and said, 'I've missed our friendship,' I didn't respond.

Now I didn't care why she'd left Israel, nor about the nature of her relationship with her son. After a brief pause, she turned the talk to everyday matters.

'So, what when the house sells? You'll be a free agent.'

'I know. A new experience.' Heath's career, my children's education and our joint assumptions had fastened me to my hometown all my life. 'I might travel for a while — see a bit of Australia. I'd like to be back in time for the baby's birth.'

'Sounds fun.'

The conversation was lagging. We really hadn't much to link us now. Without Heath, I felt as dislocated as Ruth must. We weren't so very different. Ageing women on our own, we had restricted futures. So we spoke about practical things; moving, money, work. Soon Ruth glanced at her watch and pushed back her chair.

'I'll send you my new address. You might get to Sydney. If so, do give me a call.'

'Thanks.'

'Oh, by the way . . . I still have some of Heath's music. It's in the car. Do you want it?'

'Sophie might. I'll walk out with you and collect it.'

We exchanged social smiles. Soon she was off with a casual wave. I doubted we would ever meet again. Heath and I would figure in her memories, as she would in mine. But I'd find it hard to remember why I'd been so drawn to her.

⋆　⋆　⋆

That meeting seemed to clear my path. Within a week, I received an acceptable cash offer on the house. The buyers wanted a quick settlement before Christmas. Alex helped me draw up a statement of the assets and the debts. I'd be left with enough capital to buy a small unit; the excess would meet my needs meanwhile. I'd keep favourite furniture in storage and sell the rest. I suggested Alex could buy Heath's car; I would only need a smaller model. An old friend of Heath's made an offer on the piano. With mixed feelings, I let it go.

Mrs. L. helped me with the packing. One box of Sophie's goods would be sent to Bingara. I would put the rest in storage, along with my own things. My home help eyed the essentials I would need to see me through the last weeks.

'Not much use me cummun till the final clean-up.'

I agreed to phone her. She tucked her money in her bag and we went together to her car. Parting was matter-of-fact but, as I walked back up the path alone, I knew she took with her every predictable routine I had built into my life. She tooted, waved and drove away.

* * *

My last few weeks at home were difficult. Clearing out my studio, I unearthed the clutter of unsuccessful paintings I'd stored, hoping time would provide a way to fix them. I threw out dried-up tubes of paint, stiff brushes, empty bottles of medium. It felt healthy to dispose of the past.

In the garden I'd worked so hard on, grass already grew between the paving stones and weeds were sprouting everywhere. I'd found a unit in town, and I thought of taking cuttings of some easily grown plants, then realised that I was anticipating matters. There would be an interim period between the settlements on the two properties. I'd decided to spend

Christmas with Alex and Helen and then travel North. While I saw to the last details of moving, I knew I should confront one remaining rift. I owed Rowena another chance to mend our friendship.

Nervously, for it is never pleasant to face the prospect of a slammed-down phone, I rang her several times. I was careful to choose a time when Roly would be at work, but there was never any answer. Finally I drove past her house. The curtains were drawn and a *To Let* sign explained the silence. I wondered where they'd gone — I hoped to a life that would help them through their tragedy. Sometimes there is nothing else to do but walk away and start again. In the only way I could affirm the link between us, I went to Vanessa's memorial and tied my posy to the crossbar. Only dried flowers; not my first choice but, under the circumstances, practical.

During the week when I was due to settle at the lawyers and hand over the house keys, I took a run into the city. It was a lifetime since I'd fished from the breakwater, hurled sticks into the Devil's Cauldron, or cycled past the train tracks of our town. Quite a few of the public buildings had been remodelled after the '89 earthquake. I can still remember the unreality of that morning when the earth groaned and the landscape swayed. At first I

264

didn't know what to make of it. We hadn't been exposed to the possibility of terrorist attacks in those days. The dead and the bereaved bore the brunt of that freak event. Overall, Newcastle gained from the injection of funds and jobs that brought an amazing facelift to the city. Perhaps all upheaval is eventually resolved in growth.

I had one final stop to make. In all the months since Heath's death, I'd not been back to the cemetery. Alex had tried to make me think about the wording for his father's headstone. I'd refused. So I drove out to Sandgate and found Heath's grave. For a little while I stood there, speaking to him quietly, resolving what I could between us. Alex was right. It was time we had the headstone laid. The wording would be simple, conventional, and true.

Heath Barnes, loved husband of Barbara.

★   ★   ★

Alex and Helen's help was unobtrusive, but I could see they'd agreed to make my life as sociable as possible. This would be my first Christmas without Heath, and I would have hated to spend it alone.

Alex collected me. Front yards and roof

tops were gay with cut-out Santas, sleighs, and reindeer. Strings of coloured bulbs blinked from porches and decorated the trees. Lights were strung around his front porch.

He sounded affectionate when he said, 'Helen wanted them.'

My daughter-in-law had told me he was pleased about the baby. Her pregnancy hardly showed and she looked much more relaxed. Counselling had helped resolve her guilt and worries. She had awful morning sickness, she told me; sounding almost proud of such a mundane complaint. Inside, she showed me a drawer of baby clothes, and several books on childcare. I knew the lessons she would learn through her children were not set out in any book, but held my tongue. Dear Helen; she did like to have the right equipment!

We had a simple meal that Christmas Eve. Helen was tired and went off to bed while Alex and I cleared up. He poured himself a whisky, adding a jangle of ice.

'A Christmas snifter, Mother?'

'A Moselle will do nicely.'

We took our drinks out into the tepid air of an Australian Christmas. The bass thump of party music vibrated with cicadas' shrilling. I heard laughter and smelled the sociable aroma of a neighbour's barbecue. And I sat looking at the lights, trying not to think about the rest of my life. In the face of so many endings, what ending is entirely final? Alex and Helen were surprised I had booked my trip for so soon after Christmas. The settlement on my house was proceeding smoothly, but there was still a time lag before I could move into my unit. I promised Alex and Helen that I would be back in plenty of time for my grandchild's arrival. Meanwhile I would stop in again at Bingara, to see Joe and Sophie. Then I would go where the mood took me. I had my sketch-book and pencils. Ahead waited mountains and gullies, river-beds and forests. Of course I left a share of my heart with Alex and Helen. As they saw me aboard my train, I realised just how much I cared for my edgy daughter-in-law and loved my unknowable son.

Why are you leaving us? their questioning faces seemed to ask. *Tell us where you're going?* their anxious footsteps echoed as they hurried along beside the moving carriage. I couldn't answer. They were already left behind. Ah well, it didn't matter. Later would be soon enough to say.

2006

I'm happy in my unit with its harbour view and potted terrace garden. I like being a grandmother. Twins were a surprise, but one couldn't ask for two nicer little people than my nine-year-old grandsons. When I'm not babysitting or running my part-time teaching course, I have my books and paints. It's a tranquil life of small decisions. Pansy or marigold seedlings, baked fish or steak?

It is an interview on TV that plunges me deep into the past. Looking straight at me, from one of those cosy two-seater sofas feigning intimacy beyond the range of lights and cameras, is Ruth. The novel she wrote in 2002 has been picked up and optioned for a film. It seems at last she may receive due compensation for her years of struggle. I'd read that book, *Leaving Gaza*. Now I sit riveted. She's talking about her themes; old hostilities, and how nobody wins when arbitrary action replaces negotiation. In the book, anger and vengeance were a waste. Poor little Miriam, the heroine, died for nothing, in a bungled exercise.

Ruth's giving a relaxed performance. I can't look away. Has she changed at all? There's the same throaty laugh, the challenging angle of the head, and the way she burrows through convention. It must be ten years since she left Newcastle. The events that shattered my life have apparently not affected her much. I feel a twist of unforgiving resentment. In some unyielding pocket of my heart I still blame her.

The interviewer asks why there's such a gap between books. 'You wrote your first novel in 1992,' she points out. 'Why did it take you ten years to bring out your second?'

Ruth smiles. 'Books aren't bricks,' she says. 'You don't just dump one pile and start building with another. Books arrive in their own time.'

'So what do you do in the interim? I suppose you gather material?'

Ruth seems to take the measure of this well-heeled professional. 'You gather money, and try to pay your bills. You take any work that's going and count yourself lucky, at my age. I worked as a cleaner for a while.'

The interviewer changes tack. 'Have you been home to Israel recently?'

'No.'

'No family back there you want to see?'

Ruth looks annoyed and cuts her off abruptly. 'None at all.'

So. She still hasn't forgiven Asher. How can she be so implacable towards her only child? But am I really one to talk? I've never made contact with her since she moved away. Perhaps I ought to. I could find out the telephone number of the Jewish Museum in Sydney. She might still be there. Would she want to see me? I'm a different person now.

The interview ends. For the next few weeks, I can't get her out of my mind. The major news story is the resettlement of occupied Palestinian land. The media is relentless in portraying the disregard with which soldiers move in to tear down synagogues and homes. Every night I suffer images of people trudging along, carrying their suitcases. As they board the buses I have to wonder, Where will they live? What happens to their furniture, their animals? What of their livelihoods? Their sad and stricken faces haunt me. This troubled land was Ruth's birthplace. She had to bear its struggles and, eventually, she had to leave. Once or twice I dream about her.

However, when I decide to go to Sydney, it isn't because of her. In *Spectrum*, I come across an article on Margaret Preston. A retrospective of her work has opened at the

Art Gallery of NSW. At once I resolve to go. As I have grown older, my kinship with the early Australian women painters has deepened and I include them in a module of my teaching course. Stella Bowen, Grace Cossington Smith and Mad Maggie herself went head-on with a society that refused to take women seriously as artists. As Grace put it, '*People thought that a woman painter couldn't be good. They just took it for granted.*'

I top up my coffee cup and finish reading John McDonald's thoughtful review of the Preston show. Cossington Smith was also on display. His summing up was brief and respectful. *Still they shine*. Like photographs of family, I study the coloured reproductions from the 20s — still lifes, the cityscape of Mosman Bay, the hard-edged geometry of *Implement Blue*.

Yes. I will go to Sydney. I set about checking train timetables and jot down the telephone number of the Jewish Museum.

* * *

From Central I catch a taxi to the gallery. What would all these chosen artists think, to find themselves in such a hallowed place? Most lives are anything but holy! Using a public phone, I dial the Jewish Museum. With alarming promptness, my call's transferred to the Education Unit, and I hear Ruth's voice. We arrange to meet outside the gallery at half past three. Part-pleased, part-apprehensive, I pay my fee and begin my time of contemplation with teacups; one grounded, one teetering, three on a table transformed into abstractions bound by shadows. Gladly I wander in my kind of church.

★ ★ ★

Ruth picks me up and waits while I latch the seat belt. She revs and reverses.

'Coffee? There's a sandwich bar not far from here.'

'Lovely.' I'm starving. Breakfast was a nibble of toast before I caught the early train, and I'd forgotten lunch.

'What brings you to Sydney?'

'The Preston show, mainly. Have you seen it?'

'I'm pretty busy at the moment.' She enters a snarl of traffic and I keep quiet until she finds a park in a nearby street. We walk to the sandwich shop, place our orders and find a quiet table.

Ruth's gaze is curious. I suppose mine is too. She looks older. The bone structure is sharper and gravity deepens the shadow under her jaw.

'So! What made you call the museum?'

'An impulse. I had no idea if you were still there.'

'Yes. Sydney suits me. It's where the work is. And plenty happening.'

'Unlike Newcastle.'

'I liked living there. An honest city.'

'Actually, I saw your interview on the ABC. That's what brings me here. We never properly cleared the air.'

'Cleared the air?' She seems puzzled and all at once I realise that she'd done nothing wrong. Heath had been telling the truth when he said they hadn't had an affair. I suppose a woman like Ruth doesn't play about with nuance and innuendo. She would commit herself, and clearly things had never reached that pitch with Heath. She'd enjoyed his company, but those evenings she'd spent laughing and confiding in my husband must have been no more than friendly interludes. I begin to wonder what the fuss had been about. How insecure I must have been! I let guilt and suspicion poison friendship, with far less grounds even than my poor friend Rowena, who has simply disappeared from my life. Just once, when I was waiting to cross a road, I thought I glimpsed her. The only legacy of our long friendship now is the wooden cross tethered to that new guard rail.

Ruth interrupts my thoughts. 'You were lucky to get me. Another fortnight, and I'll be gone.'

'Gone?'

'I'm going back to Israel.' She sees my look of surprise. In the interview, she made it so plain that she had no travel plans. 'It's Asher.'

The girl at the counter calls our number and we go to get our order.

'I've had a letter from him.' She tears a paper spill of sugar and in a dreamy way begins to stir the cup. 'He's ill.'

'I'm sorry. I know how close you are. Heath told me you were disappointed that he wasn't coming to Australia.' What an understatement! I'd understood she completely cut him off.

But she looks remorseful. 'I nursed my hurt feelings until quite recently. We waste a lot of time, don't we, Barb?'

'Is he still in the army?'

'He's out of all that. He's been HIV positive for several years. Now it's full-blown AIDS.' She takes another spill of sugar and stirs the cup again.

'Surely there are treatments nowadays?'

'I'm finding out what I can.'

'Is he with anyone?'

'The last relationship was messy, I gather. I don't quiz him. I need to see him. And family matters need sorting out.'

Why do we always think our children will outlive us? How lucky I am, to have been spared this particular pain. Ruth takes a sip of her coffee and gags. 'God, it's vile!'

I smile. 'You did it.'

'Did I? I gave up sugar years ago.'

'I'll get you a fresh cup.'

We stay chatting — summing up ten years of mutual living in half an hour. I remark on how cleverly in her novel she forecast the situation that dominates our television screens.

'No. *Leaving Gaza* wasn't hard to foresee, not if you've ever been part of that whole struggle. Evacuation was inevitable. Just a matter of timing.'

'I found it a sad story. Homelessness is a frightening idea.'

'Not a cosy theme.'

'What will you write about next?'

'I'm dry as a bone. I'll never make a professional. I turned down a three-book contract with my publisher because I couldn't face the deadlines. It's not that I won't. Financially it's the only way to go. But I can't.'

'Well, I can understand that.' There's every

reason to want a steady income and regular interactions with one's public, but personally I have never found creative ideas arrive to order.

Ruth drives me to Central Station. We wave, and she pulls away. Most people tread the periphery of our lives. Only our teachers enter the inner circle. They may die or leave, but we are never the same.

★ ★ ★

At home, I find a letter from Sophie. Before she went off to Europe and America, she asked me if I thought she was taking a big risk in giving up her highly-paid job in I.T.

'What if I'm unemployed when I get back, Nan?'

'Just go,' I said. 'Life has a way of running to meet you, if you take the first step.'

And it seems that's exactly what has happened. There's much talk about a certain Baltimore medical librarian who works for the Johns Hopkins Hospital. Plan all we like, these are the bolts from the blue that shape our lives. I have an intuition that Sophie will stay in Baltimore, and that it will be me, a few years from now, making the pilgrimage to meet my first great-grandchild.

I hope Joe's little girl will be a happy

woman. Nostalgic, I find an old cassette and drop it in the tape deck. Now Heath and Sophie are playing together the lovely Schubert *Fantasie in F Minor*. Heath may be dead, Sophie grown, the old piano sold; but their music remains.

I feel exhausted after my eventful day. Drawing the curtains, I take myself away to bed. Something has shifted; a space has been created. After a good night's sleep I'm awake at dawn. Old sketchbooks I glanced through recently have been gently nudging me for weeks. Now I feel the leap from thought to action. Ruth isn't alone in her fallow times. We must have life's crises to annihilate our comfort and drive our effort to understand.

It's time to get to work. As I shower and dress, yesterday seems long ago.

I'll always miss you, Ruth. We were friends, weren't we, the three of us?

I can almost hear Heath, applauding.

LOOKING FOR OLIVER

Marianne Hancock

While clearing through her late mother's bedroom, Emma finds a thirty-year-old newspaper clipping that her mother had kept, announcing the arrival of a new baby boy. Realizing that the baby must be the son she gave up for adoption, Emma finds herself vividly recalling the stigma of her schoolgirl pregnancy and the pain of her separation from the baby. She becomes transfixed by this link to her first-born, and sets out to search for Oliver, her adopted son — despite the fact that she now has a husband and two teenage children, who know nothing of her past . . .